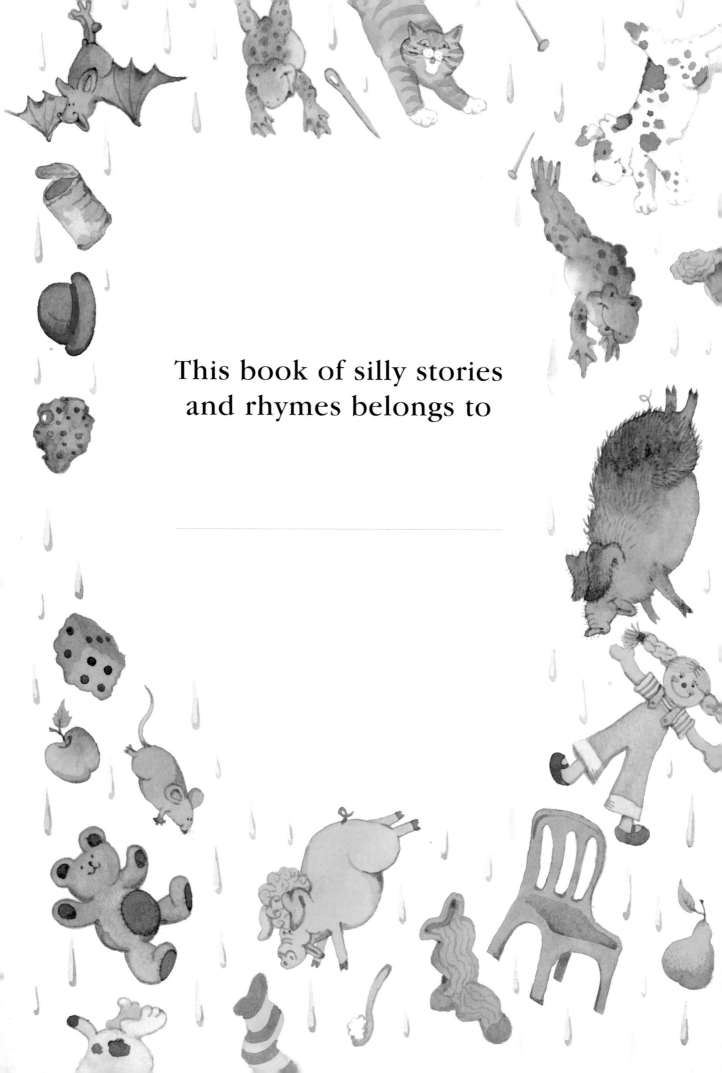

This book of silly stories
and rhymes belongs to

_____

Silly Stories

First published in 2001 by Parragon

Parragon
Queen Street House
4 Queen Street
Bath BA1 1HE

Produced by
The Templar Company plc
Pippbrook Mill, London Road
Dorking, Surrey RH4 1JE

Designed by Caroline Reeves

Printed and bound in Italy

ISBN 0 75255 670 3 Hardback
ISBN 0 75256 689 X Paperback

Silly Stories

Written by
Andy Charman, Heather Henning, Beatrice Phillpotts,
Caroline Repchuk, Louisa Somerville and Christine Tagg

Illustrated by
Diana Catchpole, Robin Edmonds, Chris Forsey
and Claire Mumford

Contents

The Incredible Centipede

Clumsy Fred

Bumping into castles,
Turning homes to rubble,
Clumsy one-eyed monster Fred
Is a load of trouble.

Ooops! There goes a lamp post!
Help! A flying shed!
When careless Fred comes into town
It fills them all with dread.

But why is Fred so clumsy?
Has he gone quite mad?
Or has the friendly monster
Just suddenly turned bad?

We must stop that creature!
But how to save the day?
A monster expert took control –
"We'll do it all my way!"

The expert went to see him.
"I do need help," he cried.
"Why am I so clumsy?
It makes me sad," he sighed.

The expert did a lot of tests,
And then he gave a cry –
"I know what's wrong with you," he said,
"The problem is your eye!"

So Fred put on a monocle,
And suddenly could see.
He wasn't clumsy any more
He was happy as could be!

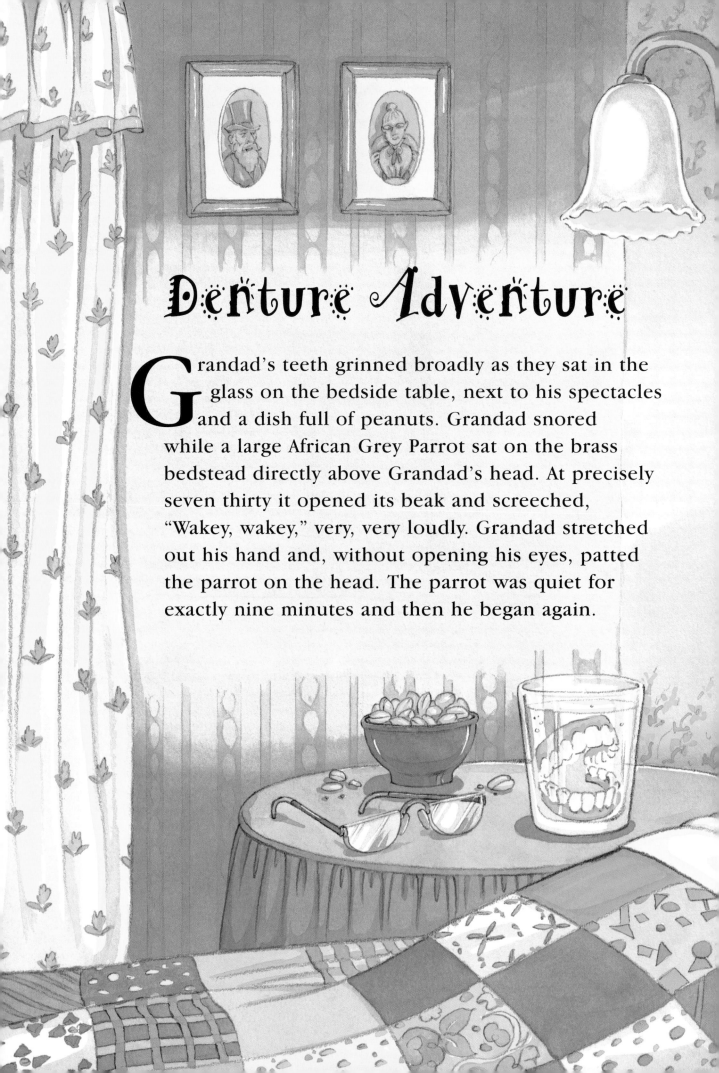

Denture Adventure

Grandad's teeth grinned broadly as they sat in the glass on the bedside table, next to his spectacles and a dish full of peanuts. Grandad snored while a large African Grey Parrot sat on the brass bedstead directly above Grandad's head. At precisely seven thirty it opened its beak and screeched, "Wakey, wakey," very, very loudly. Grandad stretched out his hand and, without opening his eyes, patted the parrot on the head. The parrot was quiet for exactly nine minutes and then he began again.

"Wakey, wakey," he called in a deafening screech. This continued until seven fifty seven when Grandad sat up in bed, yawned a gummy yawn and handed the parrot a peanut.

Grandad stumbled out of bed, put on his slippers and tripped across the hall to the bathroom. A face not unlike that of a turtle gazed back at him from the mirror, a turtle in Grandad's striped pyjamas. "Oh dear, oh dear," he said, gazing at his curious reflection. "Better put my teeth in."

Back in Grandad's bedroom, Norman the African Grey parrot had similar thoughts and was sitting proudly on the bedstead sporting Grandad's false teeth, which he had helped himself to from the glass whilst Grandad had been in the bathroom.

"Who's a pretty boy then?" he screeched

and the teeth fell out and dropped down behind the bed.

"Oh bother," said Grandad fishing around for them with the end of his best walking stick. But the teeth seemed to have vanished into thin air.

Grandma was in the kitchen making a large apple pie for tea.

"They can't have gone far," she said, as Grandad explained what had happened and, wiping her floury arms on her flowery apron, she climbed up the stairs to help him look.

"Men never look properly," she said getting down on both knees and reaching as far as she could under the big brass bed. She pulled out an old stripy sock with a hole in the toe, a furry mint humbug and a Christmas card from Auntie Beryl.

But the teeth were nowhere to be found. "Never mind," said Grandma, "I think there's an old pair in the dressing table."

There was. Grandma pulled them out triumphantly. Grandad smiled a gummy smile. "My old teeth," he said fondly and popped them into his mouth. But oh dear, oh dear, the teeth were very, very loose. They danced up and down, and wobbled from side to side and when he spoke all that came out was a *whistle, whistle, click*.

"Whistle, whistle, click!" exclaimed Norman the parrot, feeling rather proud that he had at last taught his elderly owner how to speak parrot.

"Oh well," said Grandma, on her way back down the stairs, "you'll have to get some new ones."

Grandad followed her. "Today of all days," he moaned, and put the old teeth on the kitchen table.

For the day of all days was today and today was the day of the annual village show – a very big day indeed for Grandad, who had spent several long months making a magnificent rocking horse which he had entered in one of the craft classes.

"You'll just have to not smile today," suggested Grandma not very helpfully as she lay a large pastry blanket over the fat wedges of juicy apple. "Or talk," she added. Grandad shrugged his narrow shoulders and ambled over to his potting shed, feeling rather sorry for himself.

"Hmm, I wonder," said Grandma as she gazed at the false teeth sitting on the edge of her table. She picked them up thoughtfully and then very carefully and very neatly, she crimped the edge of her apple pie with them. Grandad stood in his shed flicking a duster over the shiny dappled neck of a fine rocking horse. He stood back to admire his work. The horse was perfect in every detail. A real leather saddle and bridle, a silken mane and tail, neat glossy black hooves and two large brown eyes with wonderful long lashes. Grandad rubbed his bristly chin and frowned.

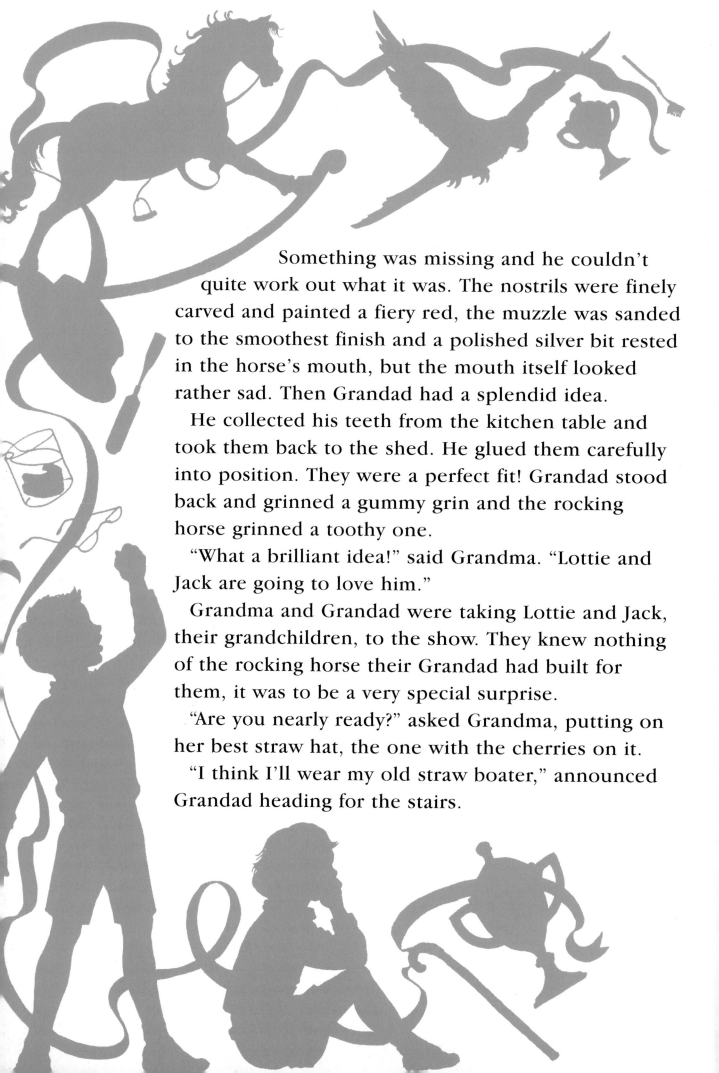

Something was missing and he couldn't quite work out what it was. The nostrils were finely carved and painted a fiery red, the muzzle was sanded to the smoothest finish and a polished silver bit rested in the horse's mouth, but the mouth itself looked rather sad. Then Grandad had a splendid idea.

He collected his teeth from the kitchen table and took them back to the shed. He glued them carefully into position. They were a perfect fit! Grandad stood back and grinned a gummy grin and the rocking horse grinned a toothy one.

"What a brilliant idea!" said Grandma. "Lottie and Jack are going to love him."

Grandma and Grandad were taking Lottie and Jack, their grandchildren, to the show. They knew nothing of the rocking horse their Grandad had built for them, it was to be a very special surprise.

"Are you nearly ready?" asked Grandma, putting on her best straw hat, the one with the cherries on it.

"I think I'll wear my old straw boater," announced Grandad heading for the stairs.

"Do hurry," called Grandma, "you don't want to be late for the judging."

Grandad knelt down and pulled out the old leather suitcase that contained his straw boater and there, lying on top of the case, were his false teeth.

"Well I never," he said, "I've got my smile back."

And Grandad needed it too. People filed past his rocking horse nodding and smiling, remarking on how well made it was and laughing out loud when they saw the teeth. Grandad felt very proud indeed.

Judging was at three o'clock precisely and Mr Pilkington-Smythe, the judge, walked back and forth twiddling his moustache thoughtfully, as he considered the many excellent entrants for the Craft Section. The standard was very high and choosing a winner was proving difficult, but eventually Mr Pilkington-Smyth stopped in front of Grandad and nodded his head. "For sheer ingenuity and a sense of humour," he said with a broad smile as he pinned the red rosette to the rocking horse and handed a delighted Grandad the fine trophy.

The crowd all cheered, everyone had wanted the rocking horse to win and none more so than Lottie and Jack who were very excited, especially as they knew the rocking horse would be coming back home to live with them.

Suddenly a photographer appeared from the local paper and asked Grandad and his family to stand around the horse.

"Smile please," he said and Grandma smiled, Lottie and Jack smiled, the rocking horse smiled, but Grandad smiled the widest smile of them all.

When the photographer had finished Lottie put her arms around the rocking horse's neck to give him a big hug then she gazed inquisitively at his mouth.

"Grandad," she asked in a puzzled voice, "are these your teeth?" Grandma laughed and Grandad bent down and very confidentially told his small granddaughter, "You should never look a gift horse in the mouth."

My Funny Family

My auntie May's got a brain like a sieve –
She forgets where the things in her kitchen all live.
There are plates in the fridge and plum jam in the jug
A chop in the teapot and carrots in the mugs!

My uncle Fred's got ears like cauliflowers –
He listens to the neighbours chat for hours and hours and hours
He can hear an ant whistling from a mile away or more
And butterflies beat their wings and tiny woodlice snore!

My cousin Bob's got eyes like a hawk –
He can see across the ocean from London to New York!
He says he can see unknown planets orbiting in space
And the moon has got a handlebar moustache upon its face.

My sister Sarah's got feet that love to dance –
She's danced from Perth to Benidorm, from Italy to France.
She dances in a dress trimmed with black and yellow lace,
Mum says she looks just like a bee and that it's a disgrace!

My brother Tom's got tricks up his sleeve –
He's got creepy things and spiders, and bugs to make you heave.
He once flicked a baked bean, which fell on Grandad's head
And dear old Grandad didn't know until he went to bed!

My dog Jasper's got a ferocious appetite –
To see him eating up his food is really quite a sight.
He wolfs down fish and chips and when he's really feeling gross,
He'll polish off a cake and several rounds of buttered toast!

The Powerful Spell

The sky went black and the villagers ran for their lives. "Help! Help!" they cried, as they dashed for the safety of the castle. "The dragon is back!" A huge shape swooped down, blotting out the sun, as the last villager flung himself inside, puffing and panting. The heavy castle doors, made of solid steel, clanged shut and the mighty bridge across the moat was drawn up.

Hovering above the thick stone castle roof and walls, its giant green, scaly wings outstretched, was a huge and terrible dragon—the enemy of the village.

With a roar of rage, the dragon opened its vast jaws and blasted the castle with its fiery breath.

Deep down below, in the castle vaults, the villagers clung together in fright. But the castle stayed firm.

"Curses!" snarled the dragon, as it flew away. "Just missed a tasty bite to eat."

The village had been a target for the dragon almost every day since it had taken up residence in the nearby mountains. Tired of dining on sheep and goats, it hankered after a nice fat villager. Fortunately, so far, it had never been quick enough to catch one.

The first time the dragon had swooped down, it was pure chance that it had not made off with a villager. It just so happened, that everyone had been invited by the king to a barbecue in the castlegrounds. Spotting a dragon coming their way, they realised at once by the bloodthirsty way it was gnashing its huge jaws that this was not a social call. With seconds to spare, they all fled to safety inside the castle

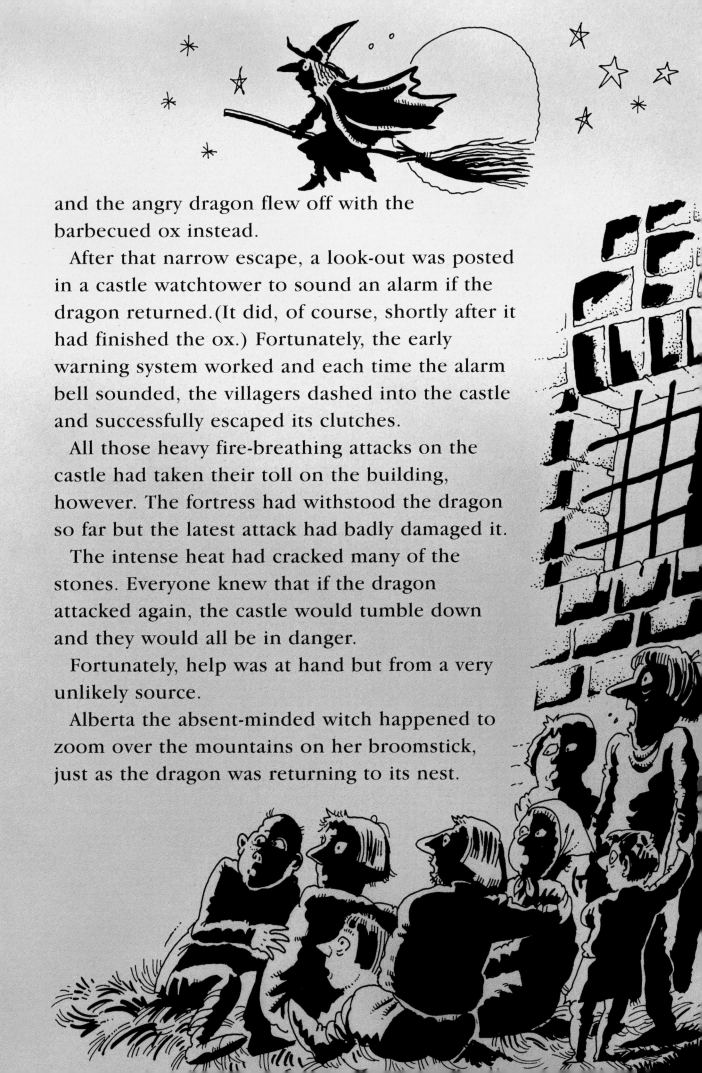

and the angry dragon flew off with the barbecued ox instead.

After that narrow escape, a look-out was posted in a castle watchtower to sound an alarm if the dragon returned. (It did, of course, shortly after it had finished the ox.) Fortunately, the early warning system worked and each time the alarm bell sounded, the villagers dashed into the castle and successfully escaped its clutches.

All those heavy fire-breathing attacks on the castle had taken their toll on the building, however. The fortress had withstood the dragon so far but the latest attack had badly damaged it.

The intense heat had cracked many of the stones. Everyone knew that if the dragon attacked again, the castle would tumble down and they would all be in danger.

Fortunately, help was at hand but from a very unlikely source.

Alberta the absent-minded witch happened to zoom over the mountains on her broomstick, just as the dragon was returning to its nest.

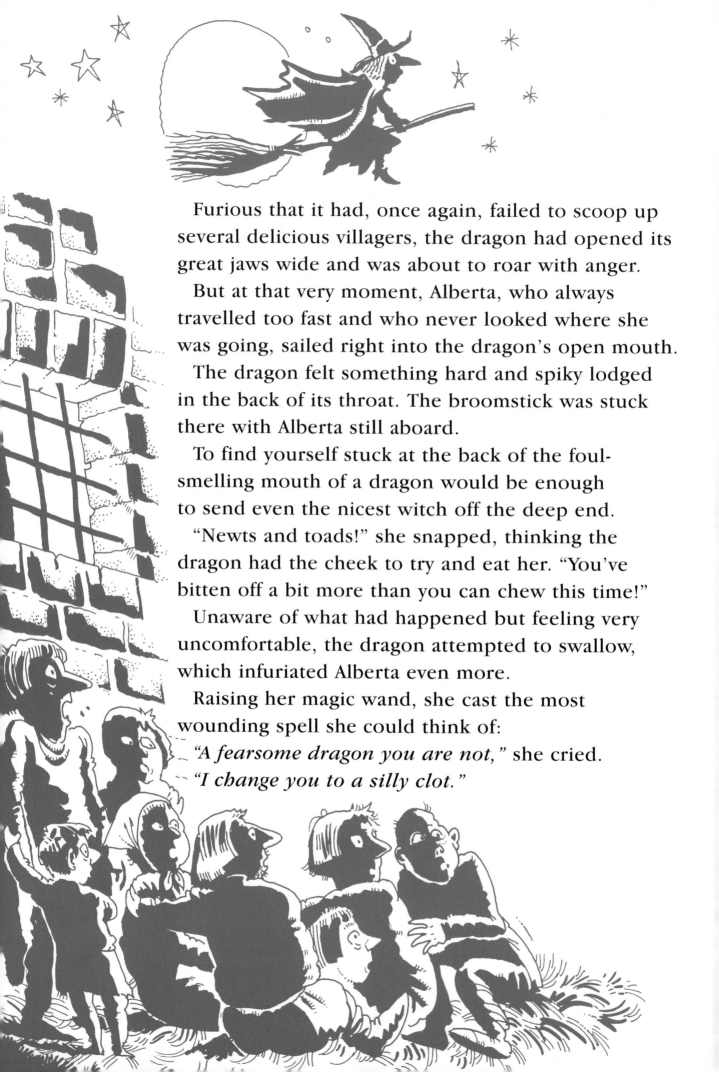

Furious that it had, once again, failed to scoop up several delicious villagers, the dragon had opened its great jaws wide and was about to roar with anger.

But at that very moment, Alberta, who always travelled too fast and who never looked where she was going, sailed right into the dragon's open mouth.

The dragon felt something hard and spiky lodged in the back of its throat. The broomstick was stuck there with Alberta still aboard.

To find yourself stuck at the back of the foul-smelling mouth of a dragon would be enough to send even the nicest witch off the deep end.

"Newts and toads!" she snapped, thinking the dragon had the cheek to try and eat her. "You've bitten off a bit more than you can chew this time!"

Unaware of what had happened but feeling very uncomfortable, the dragon attempted to swallow, which infuriated Alberta even more.

Raising her magic wand, she cast the most wounding spell she could think of:

"*A fearsome dragon you are not,*" she cried. "*I change you to a silly clot.*"

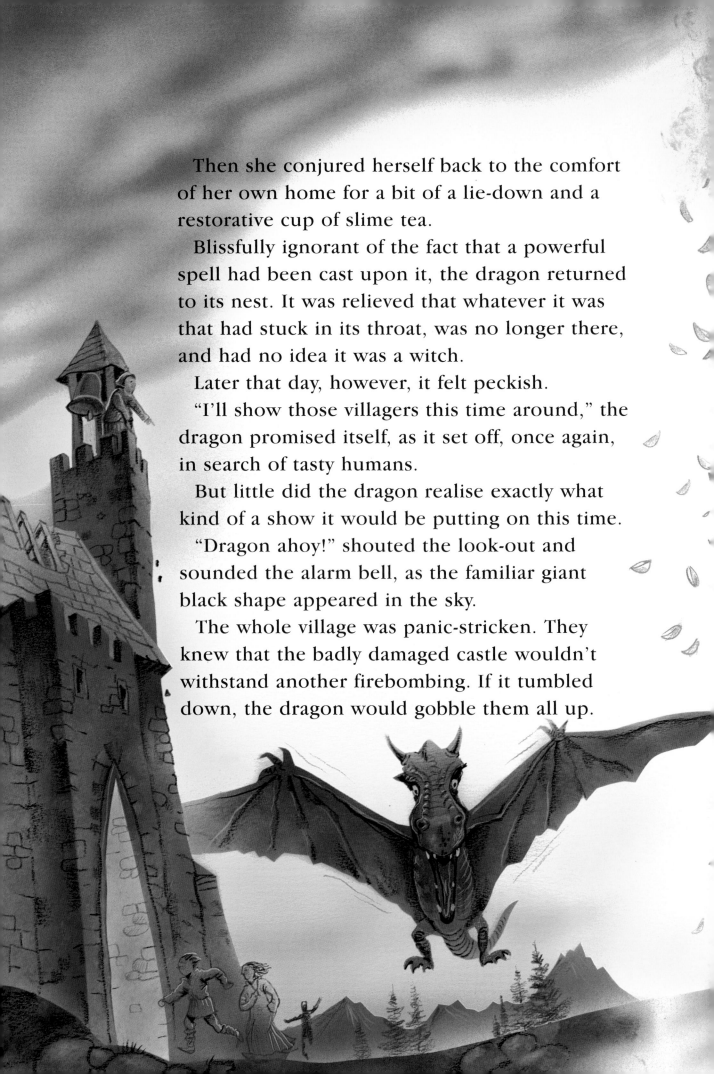

Then she conjured herself back to the comfort of her own home for a bit of a lie-down and a restorative cup of slime tea.

Blissfully ignorant of the fact that a powerful spell had been cast upon it, the dragon returned to its nest. It was relieved that whatever it was that had stuck in its throat, was no longer there, and had no idea it was a witch.

Later that day, however, it felt peckish.

"I'll show those villagers this time around," the dragon promised itself, as it set off, once again, in search of tasty humans.

But little did the dragon realise exactly what kind of a show it would be putting on this time.

"Dragon ahoy!" shouted the look-out and sounded the alarm bell, as the familiar giant black shape appeared in the sky.

The whole village was panic-stricken. They knew that the badly damaged castle wouldn't withstand another firebombing. If it tumbled down, the dragon would gobble them all up.

But there was nowhere else to run to.
So, preparing themselves for the worst,
they shut themselves up inside it, as usual.
Hidden well away from the great holes in the
roof, they clung to each other for comfort and
prayed that somehow they would be saved.

And astonishingly enough, they were.

The dreadful beating noise made by the
dragon's great wings came nearer and nearer.
The blue sky visible through the gaping holes in
the ceiling went black, as the dragon hovered
overhead. But the dreaded fiery jets of dragon
breath never came.

When the enchanted dragon drew a deep
breath and blew out with all its might, no sheets
of flame shot out. Instead, millions of sweet-
smelling flower petals fluttered downwards
from its gaping jaws.

The villagers stared in amazement, as pretty
petals floated through the holes above their
heads and gathered in drifts around their feet.

Scarcely able to believe its eyes, either, the dragon gazed in horror at the beautiful blossom heaped below.

Drawing a second deeper breath, the dragon attempted to obliterate all that beauty with the biggest firebolt it had ever produced. But this time, showers of delicious chocolates rained down on the castle, fell through the cracks in the ceiling and collected in heaps on the floor around the villagers.

The furious dragon gave a great roar of anguish but Alberta's spell ensured that something just as silly as the flowers and chocolates emerged from its fearsome-looking jaws.

Instead of a spine-chilling bellow, the dragon started to yodel in a deep, rich baritone and found to its great embarrassment that it couldn't stop.

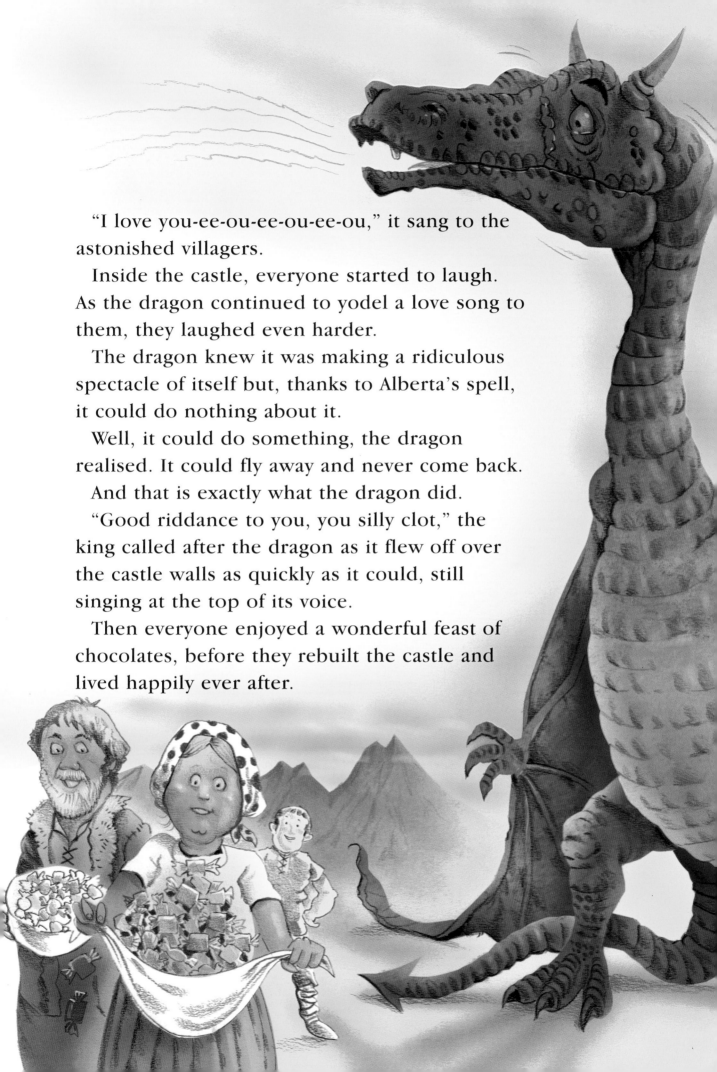

"I love you-ee-ou-ee-ou-ee-ou," it sang to the astonished villagers.

Inside the castle, everyone started to laugh. As the dragon continued to yodel a love song to them, they laughed even harder.

The dragon knew it was making a ridiculous spectacle of itself but, thanks to Alberta's spell, it could do nothing about it.

Well, it could do something, the dragon realised. It could fly away and never come back.

And that is exactly what the dragon did.

"Good riddance to you, you silly clot," the king called after the dragon as it flew off over the castle walls as quickly as it could, still singing at the top of its voice.

Then everyone enjoyed a wonderful feast of chocolates, before they rebuilt the castle and lived happily ever after.

The Incredible Centipede

I'm not just an ordinary centipede,
 I live in a circus van,
 The top performers are known to me
And I have a wonderful plan…

We'll reach a town, and as the sun goes down
The folks will crowd the tent;
With music to thrill, they'll pick up the bill
And read with astonishment:

'Star of the show in the ring tonight
And we hope he does succeed,
Is the enterprising, most surprising
Incredible Centipede!'

The curtains will part and out I'll dart
And shake a leg or six,
Then in spangled tights I'll scale the heights
To perform my amazing tricks.

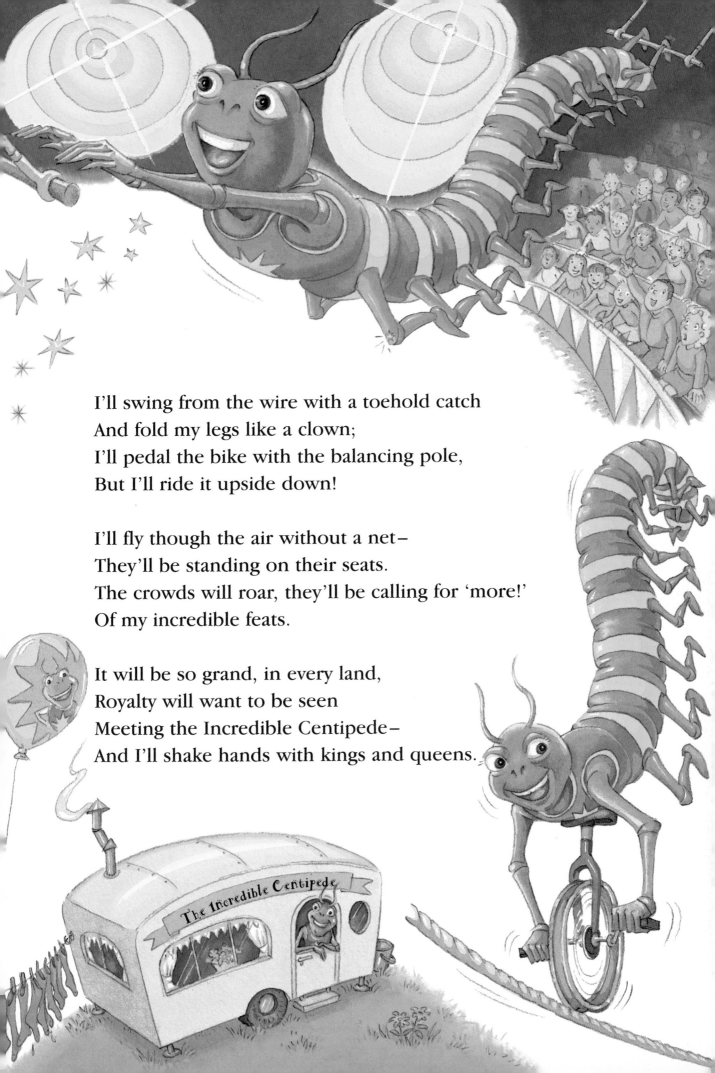

I'll swing from the wire with a toehold catch
And fold my legs like a clown;
I'll pedal the bike with the balancing pole,
But I'll ride it upside down!

I'll fly though the air without a net–
They'll be standing on their seats.
The crowds will roar, they'll be calling for 'more!'
Of my incredible feats.

It will be so grand, in every land,
Royalty will want to be seen
Meeting the Incredible Centipede–
And I'll shake hands with kings and queens.

Silly Jill

There was once a girl called Jill Martin and she always thought she knew best. Once, she took pity on a gorilla at her local zoo. She decided he would much rather live with her, than with his wife and babies in the jungle-like park that had been designed especially for them. So, one night, she crept into the zoo and lured him out of his lovely cage with bunches of bananas, while his family was sleeping.

They caught a night bus back to her house and
when the conductor made a fuss and said it was
against the rules to carry huge apes, Jill told him
not to be so silly and threatened to report him.
But the gorilla would not sit still. He leapt from seat
to seat and drummed his chest until the bus shook.
The driver called him a public nuisance and drove
him straight back to the zoo. Everyone could see he
would be much happier there – except Jill.

Whenever anyone tried to stop her from doing
anything, Jill would simply reply, "Oh, don't be so
silly, I know exactly what I'm doing." She would go
ahead and do it and quite often the results were
disastrous. No-one tried to stop Jill from doing silly
things at home, which made her even worse. She was
an only child and she could do no wrong in the eyes
of her mother and father. They spoilt her horribly
and always agreed with everything she said.

When Jill's parents took her to the circus for her
birthday and she insisted that she could do the

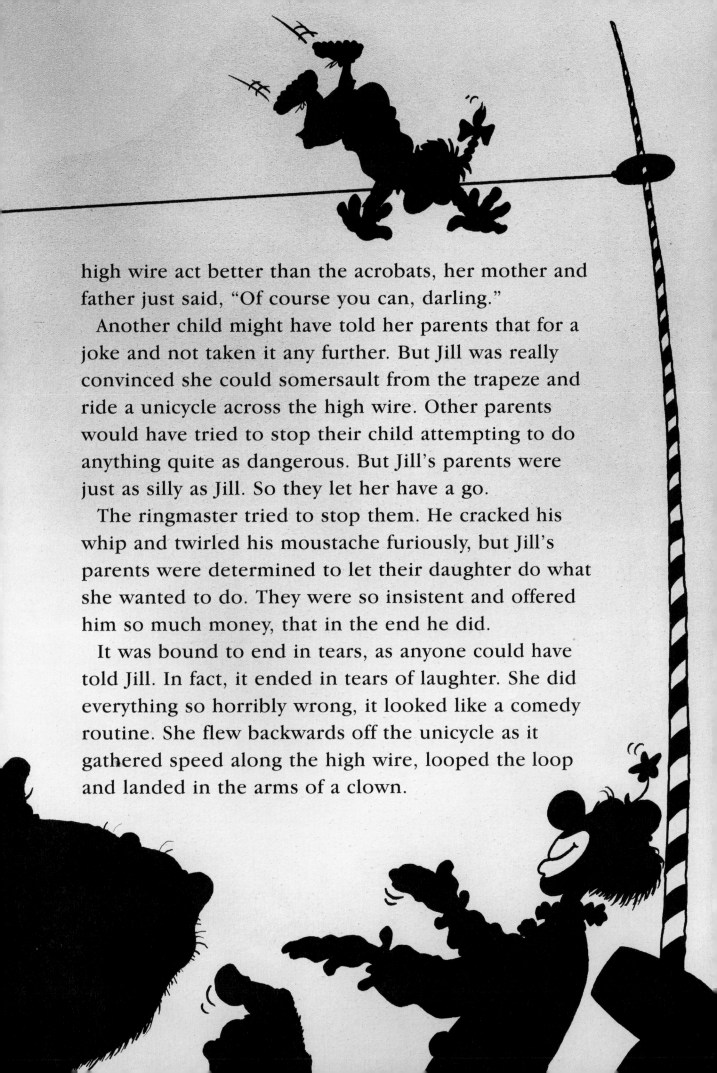

high wire act better than the acrobats, her mother and father just said, "Of course you can, darling."

Another child might have told her parents that for a joke and not taken it any further. But Jill was really convinced she could somersault from the trapeze and ride a unicycle across the high wire. Other parents would have tried to stop their child attempting to do anything quite as dangerous. But Jill's parents were just as silly as Jill. So they let her have a go.

The ringmaster tried to stop them. He cracked his whip and twirled his moustache furiously, but Jill's parents were determined to let their daughter do what she wanted to do. They were so insistent and offered him so much money, that in the end he did.

It was bound to end in tears, as anyone could have told Jill. In fact, it ended in tears of laughter. She did everything so horribly wrong, it looked like a comedy routine. She flew backwards off the unicycle as it gathered speed along the high wire, looped the loop and landed in the arms of a clown.

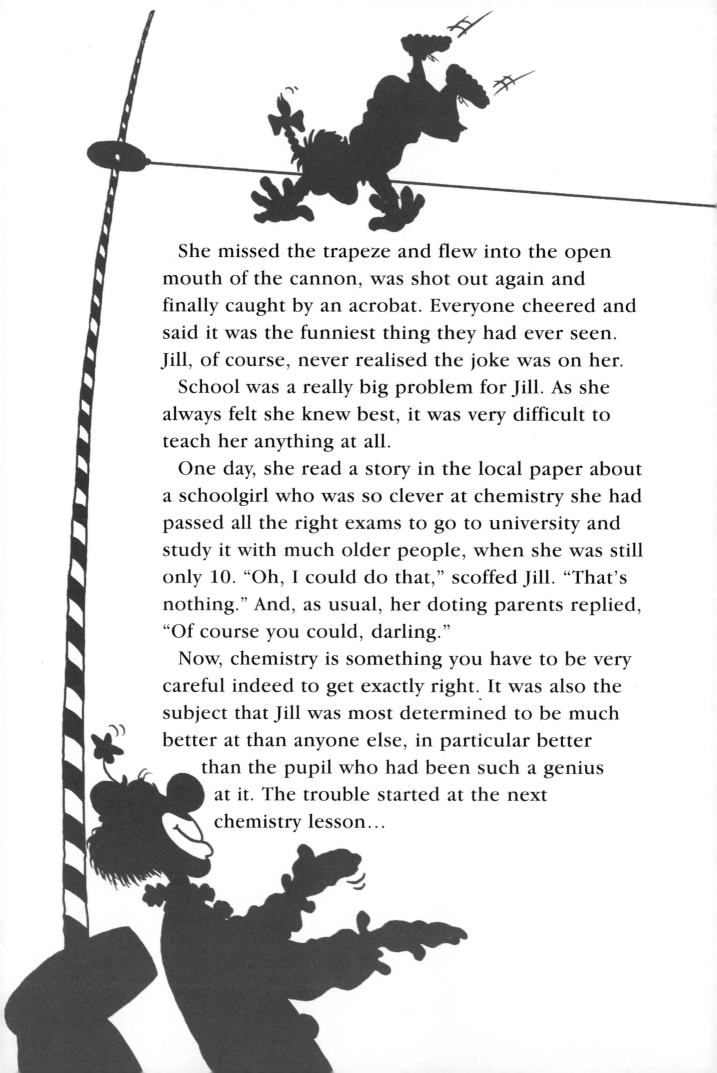

She missed the trapeze and flew into the open mouth of the cannon, was shot out again and finally caught by an acrobat. Everyone cheered and said it was the funniest thing they had ever seen. Jill, of course, never realised the joke was on her.

School was a really big problem for Jill. As she always felt she knew best, it was very difficult to teach her anything at all.

One day, she read a story in the local paper about a schoolgirl who was so clever at chemistry she had passed all the right exams to go to university and study it with much older people, when she was still only 10. "Oh, I could do that," scoffed Jill. "That's nothing." And, as usual, her doting parents replied, "Of course you could, darling."

Now, chemistry is something you have to be very careful indeed to get exactly right. It was also the subject that Jill was most determined to be much better at than anyone else, in particular better than the pupil who had been such a genius at it. The trouble started at the next chemistry lesson…

The rest of the class listened carefully to the chemistry teacher. She explained that in their next experiment it was very important not to mix the wrong liquids. Under no circumstances should blue be mixed with red.

'Huh!' thought Jill. 'I bet it works much better if you mix the blue with the red.' And so, without anyone seeing, she mixed blue and red.

Bang! Jill's flask exploded the moment they were combined and a stream of foul-smelling, smoking purple liquid poured onto the carpet.

"You silly, silly girl!" shouted the chemistry teacher. "What have you done?"

It was difficult to see exactly what Jill had done, the classroom was so full of smoke.

But everyone started to feel what she had done almost immediately.

"Help!" they shouted, as one by one, they felt themselves being lifted off the floor.

A most extraordinary thing had happened. The spilt liquid had made the pile of the carpet grow like grass. Only, instead of growing slowly like grass normally does, the carpet was growing upwards in leaps and bounds, like a meadow that had gone mad.

"Make for the door!" screamed the chemistry teacher, as the long waving pile of the classroom carpet carried them all up towards the ceiling. It was rather like being on a rollercoaster.

So they all did, even Jill. They crawled across the narrow space that was still left as fast as they could, trying not to knock their heads on the lights, while the whole carpet shot upwards in a great mass.

Then, just before they reached the door, the carpet flowered. Fat buds burst out into brightly coloured blooms. Everyone who suffered from hay fever, spluttered and sneezed.

Luckily, the classroom door was open. They squeezed their way through it before the carpet filled the room and then tumbled out into the corridor, chasing the last pupils out of the door.

"Run for it!" commanded the teacher, pressing the fire alarm to alert the rest of the school. And eight hundred pupils, including Jill, thirty members of staff, the caretaker and the cat raced for the safety of the playground, just before the school was completely swallowed up by carpet.

It took every fireman in the town a week to cut the carpet down and for months afterwards it still sprouted the occasional flower.

The school had to be closed, of course, while the giant carpet was scythed, mowed, rolled and finally brought under control. The head teacher was furious with Jill, when she heard how it had all started.

"Your silly, thoughtless behaviour could have destroyed my school and everyone in it," she told her. "I hope this has taught you a lesson and you know now that you do not always know better than anyone else."

Fortunately for Jill – and the school – it had taught her a lesson that she never forgot. From that dreadful day onwards, she stopped insisting she knew best and to everyone's relief, there were no more disasters.

In fact, Jill's terrible mistake turned out to be a fantastic opportunity for the school. An army chief heard about Jill's silly experiment and the amazing result. He decided that a quick-growing carpet would be an excellent weapon. He paid the school a lot of money for the details of Jill's purple mixture. This meant that the school was able to build a swimming pool, ice rink and bowling centre for everyone in the town. And it wasn't long before Jill mended her ways and really did become a star pupil – but everyone still knew her as Silly Jill!

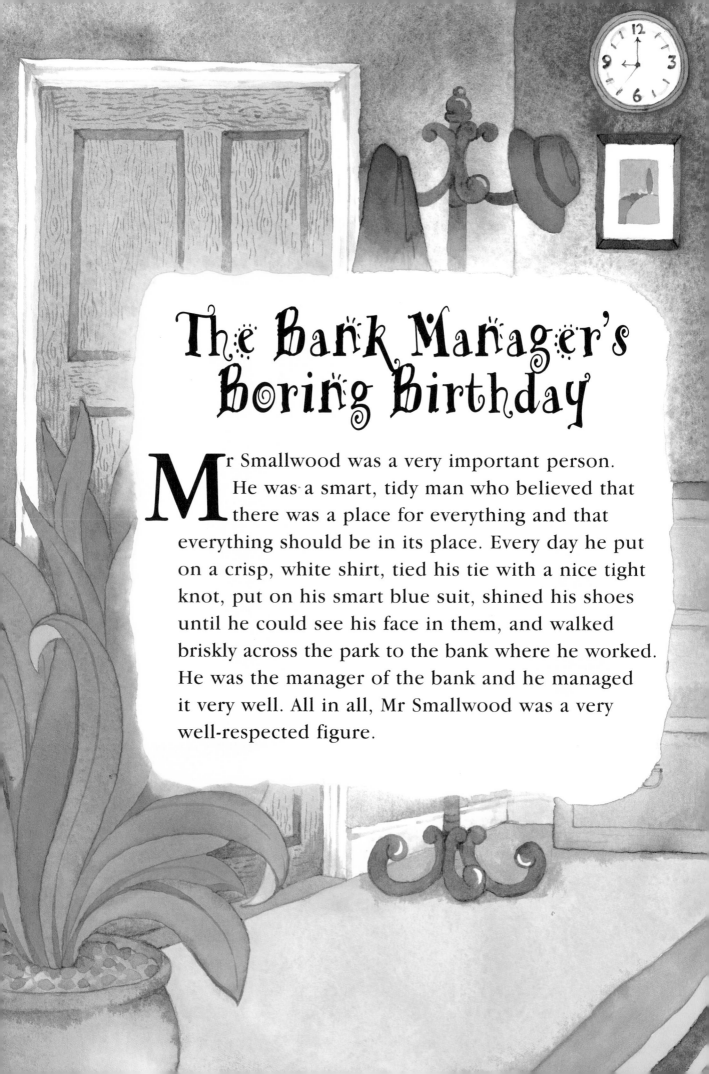

The Bank Manager's Boring Birthday

Mr Smallwood was a very important person. He was a smart, tidy man who believed that there was a place for everything and that everything should be in its place. Every day he put on a crisp, white shirt, tied his tie with a nice tight knot, put on his smart blue suit, shined his shoes until he could see his face in them, and walked briskly across the park to the bank where he worked. He was the manager of the bank and he managed it very well. All in all, Mr Smallwood was a very well-respected figure.

Now, as you can imagine, Mr Smallwood didn't take very many days off, but he thought his birthday should be one of them. However, he didn't like sitting at home much, because there was nothing to do. His bed was made; his dishes were washed and dried and put away; his socks were in the drawer marked 'socks'; and he'd read all of his books. Everything was in its place. With a sigh he realized he missed the bank. Then the telephone rang.

"Good morning," he said. "Mr Joseph Smallwood speaking. How can I help you?" And then,"Yes, of course. Certainly. I'll be along straight away." He put the telephone down and smiled. Just as he thought– they needed him at the bank. They couldn't manage without him.

Hurriedly, Mr Smallwood put on his shirt and tie, and his neat blue suit and stepped out into the street. Not such a boring birthday after all! It was a bright, sunny morning, the birds were singing in the trees, the traffic warden was

writing tickets, the cars were at a standstill.
Everything was as it should be. A perfectly
ordinary day.

Mr Smallwood hadn't gone far when he came
across a pig.

"Now that's not the right place for a pig,"
said Mr Smallwood. "I should catch that
animal and take it to the market." So he chased
the pig into the park. But the pig had other
ideas. With an excited squeal, it dashed off to
hide in the rose bushes. Mr Smallwood
made a daring leap. He flew gracefully through
the air and stretching out his arms he caught the
pig. Then with a loud THWUMP! they landed in
a large, smelly heap of horse manure.

"Golly!" said Mr Smallwood, as he stood up.
The front of his suit and his glasses were
covered with horse manure, but the pig was
safely in his arms.

Mr Smallwood set off rather slowly across
the park in the direction of the market.

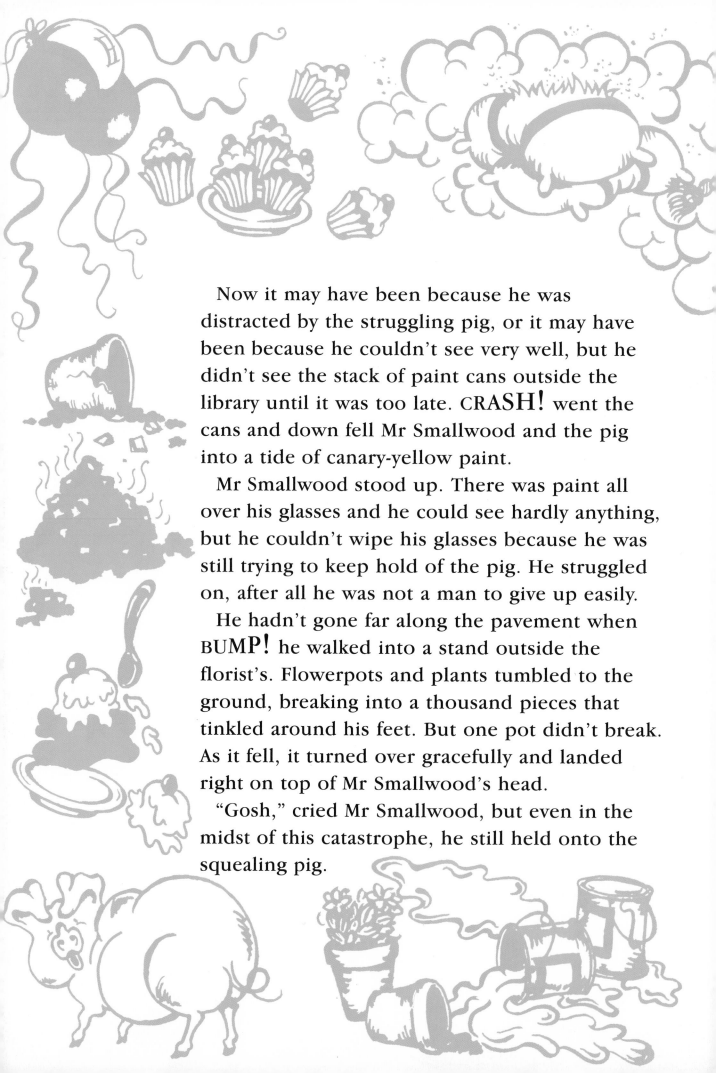

Now it may have been because he was distracted by the struggling pig, or it may have been because he couldn't see very well, but he didn't see the stack of paint cans outside the library until it was too late. CRASH! went the cans and down fell Mr Smallwood and the pig into a tide of canary-yellow paint.

Mr Smallwood stood up. There was paint all over his glasses and he could see hardly anything, but he couldn't wipe his glasses because he was still trying to keep hold of the pig. He struggled on, after all he was not a man to give up easily.

He hadn't gone far along the pavement when BUMP! he walked into a stand outside the florist's. Flowerpots and plants tumbled to the ground, breaking into a thousand pieces that tinkled around his feet. But one pot didn't break. As it fell, it turned over gracefully and landed right on top of Mr Smallwood's head.

"Gosh," cried Mr Smallwood, but even in the midst of this catastrophe, he still held onto the squealing pig.

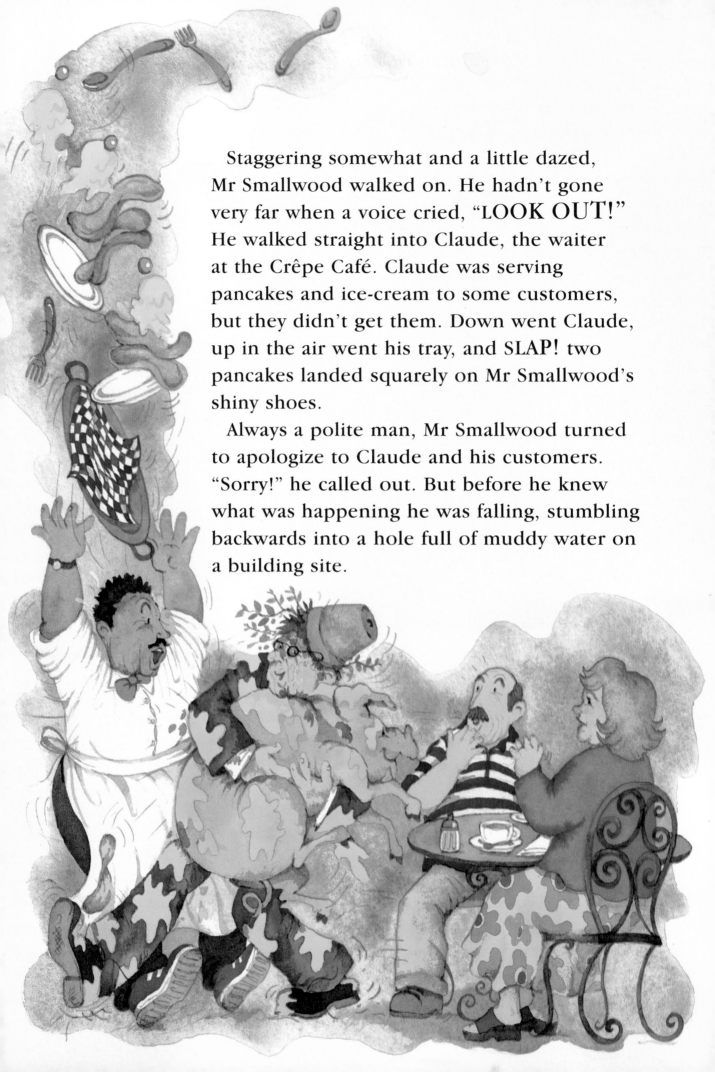

Staggering somewhat and a little dazed, Mr Smallwood walked on. He hadn't gone very far when a voice cried, "LOOK OUT!" He walked straight into Claude, the waiter at the Crêpe Café. Claude was serving pancakes and ice-cream to some customers, but they didn't get them. Down went Claude, up in the air went his tray, and SLAP! two pancakes landed squarely on Mr Smallwood's shiny shoes.

Always a polite man, Mr Smallwood turned to apologize to Claude and his customers. "Sorry!" he called out. But before he knew what was happening he was falling, stumbling backwards into a hole full of muddy water on a building site.

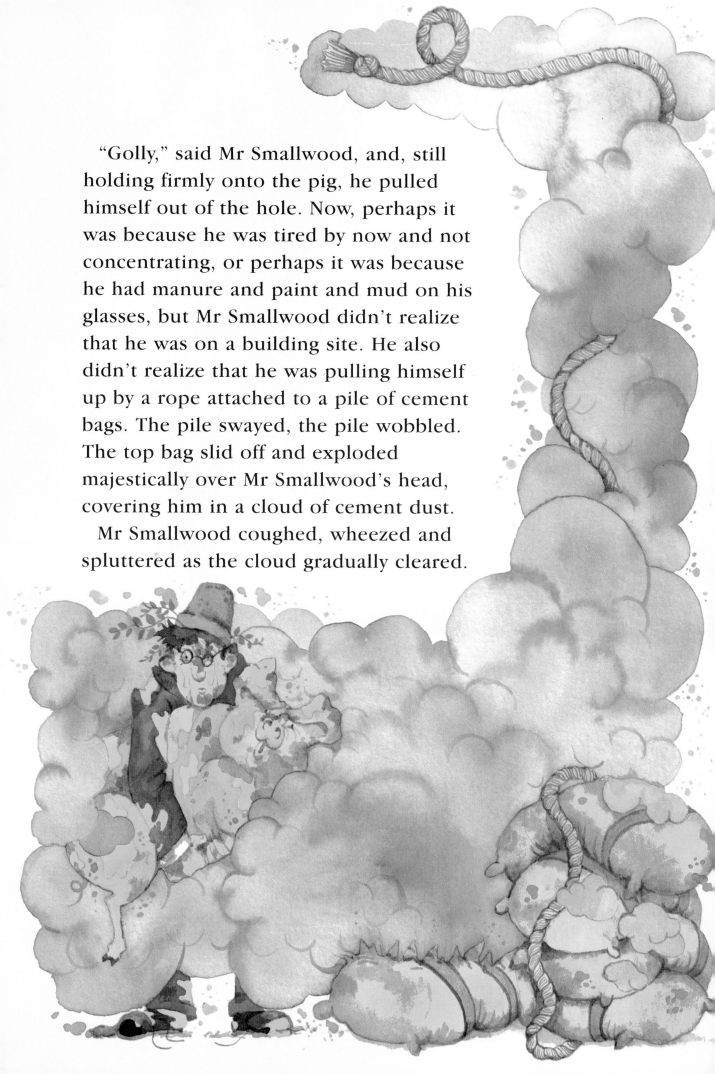

"Golly," said Mr Smallwood, and, still holding firmly onto the pig, he pulled himself out of the hole. Now, perhaps it was because he was tired by now and not concentrating, or perhaps it was because he had manure and paint and mud on his glasses, but Mr Smallwood didn't realize that he was on a building site. He also didn't realize that he was pulling himself up by a rope attached to a pile of cement bags. The pile swayed, the pile wobbled. The top bag slid off and exploded majestically over Mr Smallwood's head, covering him in a cloud of cement dust.

Mr Smallwood coughed, wheezed and spluttered as the cloud gradually cleared.

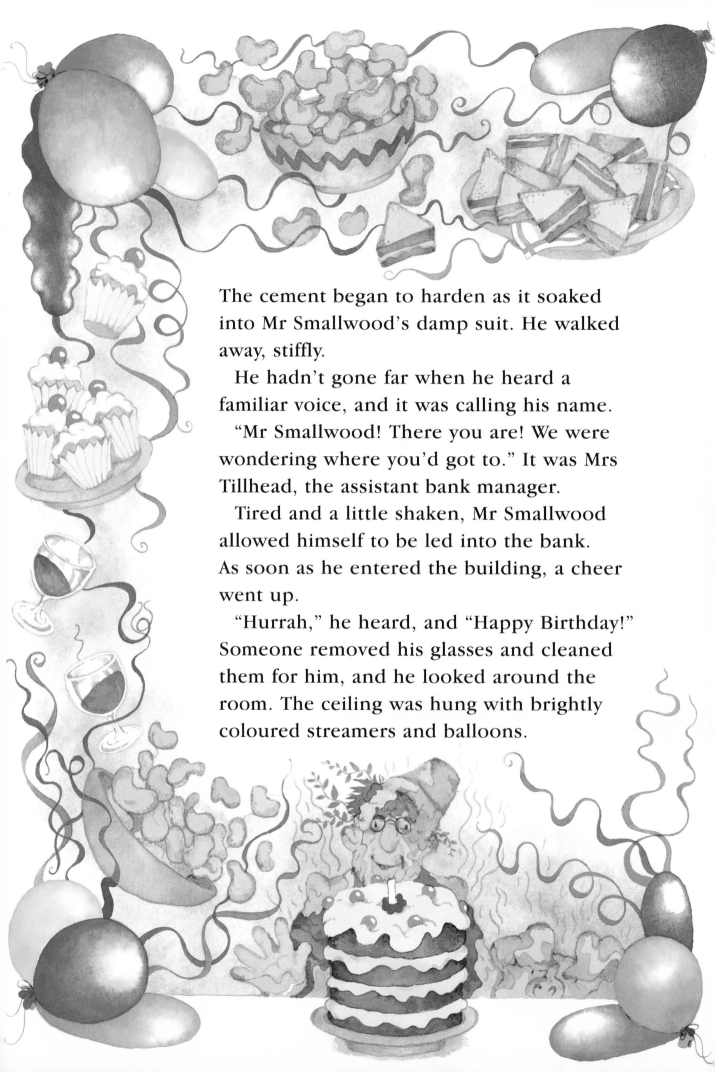

The cement began to harden as it soaked
into Mr Smallwood's damp suit. He walked
away, stiffly.

He hadn't gone far when he heard a
familiar voice, and it was calling his name.

"Mr Smallwood! There you are! We were
wondering where you'd got to." It was Mrs
Tillhead, the assistant bank manager.

Tired and a little shaken, Mr Smallwood
allowed himself to be led into the bank.
As soon as he entered the building, a cheer
went up.

"Hurrah," he heard, and "Happy Birthday!"
Someone removed his glasses and cleaned
them for him, and he looked around the
room. The ceiling was hung with brightly
coloured streamers and balloons.

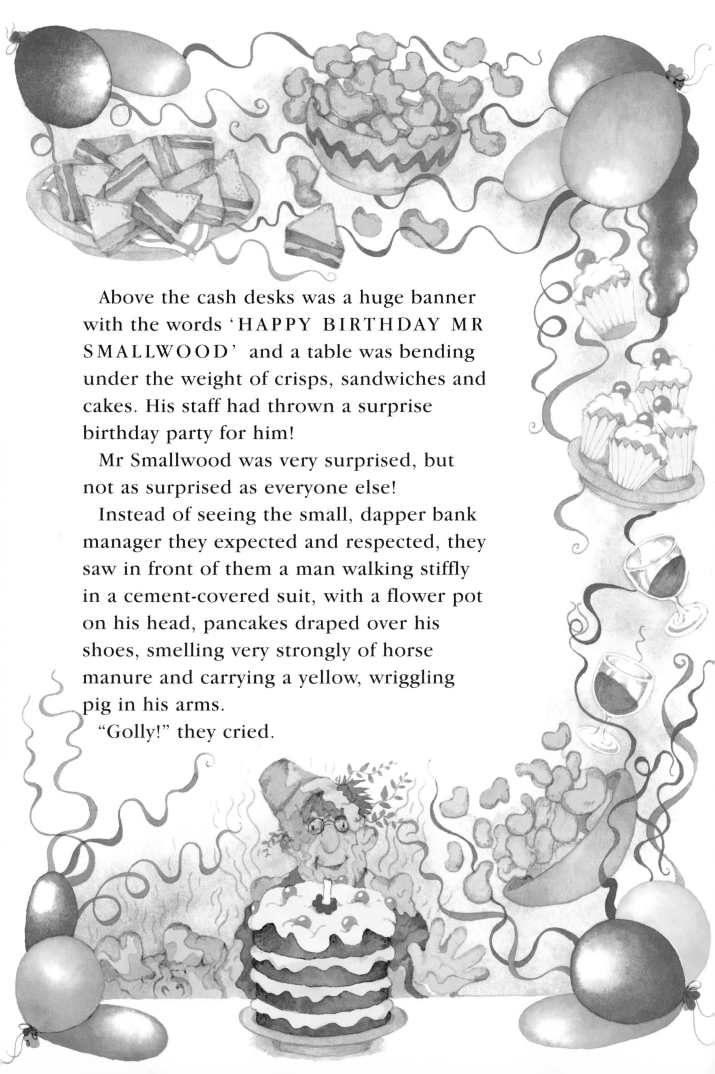

Above the cash desks was a huge banner with the words 'HAPPY BIRTHDAY MR SMALLWOOD' and a table was bending under the weight of crisps, sandwiches and cakes. His staff had thrown a surprise birthday party for him!

Mr Smallwood was very surprised, but not as surprised as everyone else!

Instead of seeing the small, dapper bank manager they expected and respected, they saw in front of them a man walking stiffly in a cement-covered suit, with a flower pot on his head, pancakes draped over his shoes, smelling very strongly of horse manure and carrying a yellow, wriggling pig in his arms.

"Golly!" they cried.

The Land Where Animals Rule

In the land where the animals rule,
The children don't go to school.
They live on farms, and flap their arms,
Just like the chickens used to do.

The post-bears always wear blue,
It's faster on four legs than two.
But it's always better to send it by letter,
Because packets tend to get chewed.

Jaguars and speeding cheetahs,
Are stopped when they go too fast
By policing cats, in pointed hats,
And pandas in people-coloured cars.

Horses take themselves for a ride,
They trot down the road side by side.
In the carriages they own they travel alone,
There's no room for two on the inside.

In restaurants where herbivores go,
They never eat meat so I'm told.
Cows do the cooking while no-one is looking,
It's grass, and it's usually cold.

If you go for a round-the-world sail
You travel on the back of a whale.
Hold on for dear life when he starts to dive,
And look out for that over-sized tail.

It's fun where the animals rule,
No-one tells you what you ought to do.
Their idea of fun is to sleep in the sun,
It's just the place for a person like you.

The Emperor's New Nose

"AAchoooo!" The emperor spluttered and wheezed into his enormous white handkerchief, as he blew his sore and throbbing nose for the umpteenth time that day. To say that the emperor had a cold would be the understatement of the year. This was the cold to beat all colds. An all-coughing, all-sneezing, all-spluttering and all-wheezing type of cold. A real throat-aching, eye-watering, bone-shaking, head rattler. Get the picture?

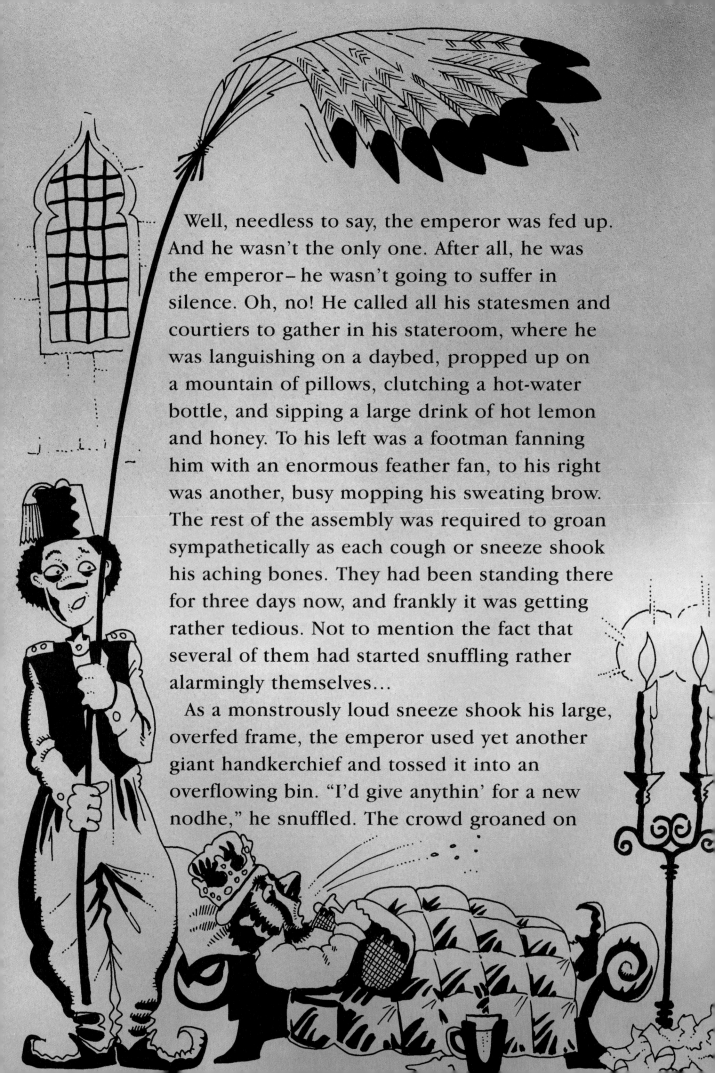

Well, needless to say, the emperor was fed up.
And he wasn't the only one. After all, he was
the emperor– he wasn't going to suffer in
silence. Oh, no! He called all his statesmen and
courtiers to gather in his stateroom, where he
was languishing on a daybed, propped up on
a mountain of pillows, clutching a hot-water
bottle, and sipping a large drink of hot lemon
and honey. To his left was a footman fanning
him with an enormous feather fan, to his right
was another, busy mopping his sweating brow.
The rest of the assembly was required to groan
sympathetically as each cough or sneeze shook
his aching bones. They had been standing there
for three days now, and frankly it was getting
rather tedious. Not to mention the fact that
several of them had started snuffling rather
alarmingly themselves…

As a monstrously loud sneeze shook his large,
overfed frame, the emperor used yet another
giant handkerchief and tossed it into an
overflowing bin. "I'd give anythin' for a new
nodhe," he snuffled. The crowd groaned on

cue with as much sympathy as they could muster. But the court jester, who was worn to a frazzle with his attempts to entertain the ailing Emperor, pricked up his ears at once.

"A new nose! What a marvellous idea. Why ever didn't I think of it myself? And you'd really give anything for a new nose?" the court jester said, smiling slyly.

"Anythin'!" wheezed the emperor. "If only it were possible."

"Anything is possible, your Majesty," smiled the court jester mysteriously, bowing low.

Now it just so happened that the court jester had had his eye on the emperor's fair daughter, Bella, for quite some time. She was rather taken with him too, she liked his sense of humour. There was just one problem – emperors didn't like their daughters marrying jesters. It wasn't good for the image, having a son-in-law that people laughed at. But, as the emperor had given his word in front of his entire court to grant any wish, the jester knew he would find it hard to wriggle out of his commitment.

So, sensing the opportunity to claim Bella as his bride, he set to work at once to transform the emperor's sickly nose.

Taking out his bag of tricks, his book of spells, and his magic wand, the court jester rubbed his chin thoughtfully. As far as court jesters go, he was a pretty good all-rounder. He had a repertoire of jokes for all occasions, was a master of silly walks, an expert at juggling, fire-eating and tightrope walking. A dab hand at card tricks, and not too bad at magic. But not too good, either, as the emperor was about to find out!

After several minutes spent looking through his book of spells, the court jester came upon just the thing. 'Transformation of body parts. Difficulty rating– four star. Not for the inexperienced or faint-hearted.' Well, it was a bit too difficult, but a lot was at stake, and without further ado, he decided to give it a go.

Word soon spread amongst the courtiers of the impending transformation spell. This should liven things up a bit! An excited hush fell on the room, as the jester set up sparkly purple curtains around the emperor.

The jester paced up and down, muttering under his breath. He was deciding on the exact wording of the spell and practising until he was word perfect. Then, he picked up his wand, tapped it on his spell book, and asked for silence as he recited the magic words:

"Abracadabra, snuffles and wheezes,
Away with this nose with its splutters and sneezes.
Something grand and imposing appear in its place,
A noble nose, fit for a true leader's face!"

With that, he waved his wand in the air, making a trail of sparkling stars. Behind the screen, there was a bright green flash of light, and the audience let out a great gasp as the court jester pulled back the curtains to reveal the emperor with his new nose in all its glory. It was certainly grand, certainly imposing, and quite likely fit for a noble leader– so long as he was leading a herd of elephants! For there, right in the middle of the emperor's startled and alarmed face, was none other than an elephant's long, twisty trunk!

Well, what a commotion broke out! At first the courtiers were stunned into silence. Then there was a great hullaballoo, since, not knowing whether to laugh or cry, they bombarded the secretly astonished and horrified court jester with questions. I say secretly, because although his magic was not up to much, he was ever the professional, and was not about to let on for one moment that this was anything other than he had intended. He was also well aware that emperors are notoriously easy to fool, and luckily for him, this one was no exception.

"Your Majesty!" he exclaimed bowing low. "I am delighted to report a complete success! What a noble and distinctive nose, what an exceptionally unique profile. Doesn't he look marvellous?" The court jester turned to the courtiers, who, anxious not to offend the emperor, all loudly declared their approval!

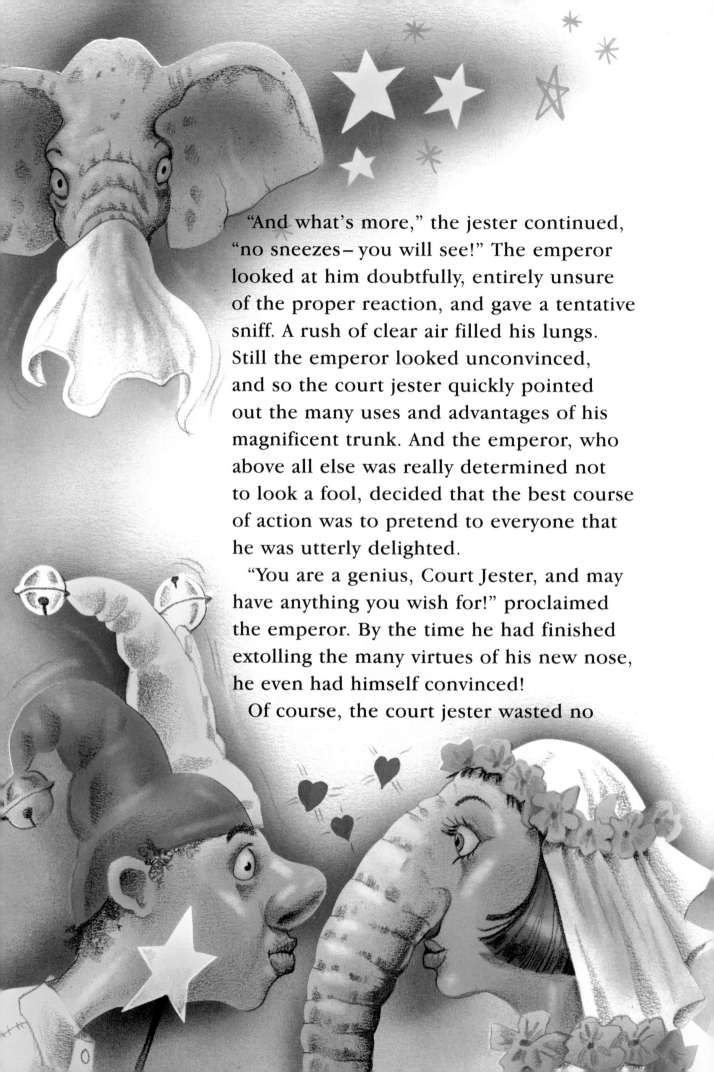

"And what's more," the jester continued, "no sneezes– you will see!" The emperor looked at him doubtfully, entirely unsure of the proper reaction, and gave a tentative sniff. A rush of clear air filled his lungs. Still the emperor looked unconvinced, and so the court jester quickly pointed out the many uses and advantages of his magnificent trunk. And the emperor, who above all else was really determined not to look a fool, decided that the best course of action was to pretend to everyone that he was utterly delighted.

"You are a genius, Court Jester, and may have anything you wish for!" proclaimed the emperor. By the time he had finished extolling the many virtues of his new nose, he even had himself convinced!

Of course, the court jester wasted no

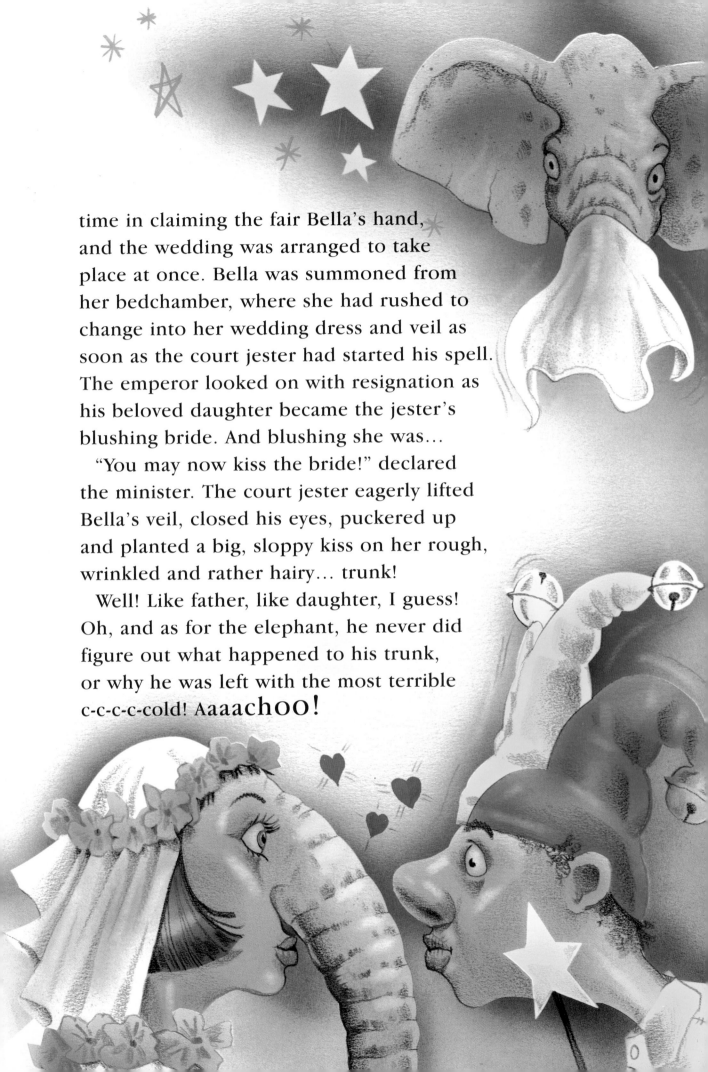

time in claiming the fair Bella's hand, and the wedding was arranged to take place at once. Bella was summoned from her bedchamber, where she had rushed to change into her wedding dress and veil as soon as the court jester had started his spell. The emperor looked on with resignation as his beloved daughter became the jester's blushing bride. And blushing she was...

"You may now kiss the bride!" declared the minister. The court jester eagerly lifted Bella's veil, closed his eyes, puckered up and planted a big, sloppy kiss on her rough, wrinkled and rather hairy... trunk!

Well! Like father, like daughter, I guess! Oh, and as for the elephant, he never did figure out what happened to his trunk, or why he was left with the most terrible c-c-c-c-cold! Aaaachoo!

A Shipful of Fun

It was a wild, stormy night, windows rattled and dustbin lids clattered down the narrow streets. Poppy sat wide awake in her bed, listening to the wind howling and the crashing waves. She wondered about the poor seagulls – where would they go on a night like this? Suddenly, her room was filled with bright orange light. A flare! Something was happening at sea! Poppy woke her father and they rushed down to the beach, pulling on their coats. People were appearing from everywhere and there was an air of anticipation as they all gathered on the beach – Poppy had the feeling it would be an eventful night.

Out on the raging sea, Captain Thomas clung to the bow of his lurching ship and shot another flare into the sky. As it lit up the stormy sky, he could see in the orange glow the townspeople gathered on the beach. He was relieved to see the lifeboat being hauled down the slipway and into the crashing waves. He was all alone on his stricken ship and it was heading for the rocks. But the lifeboat was coming, bobbing steadfastly towards him.

Captain Thomas jumped into the foaming water and swam towards the lifeboat. He went under for a second and came up spluttering and coughing, then strong hands grabbed him and stronger arms pulled him into the boat.

"Thank you, thank you," he gasped. The boat turned and took him to the shore. There was a horrible crunching sound as his ship hit the rocks, then it rolled onto its side.

In the morning, Poppy went down to the beach to look at the ship. The sea was calm now, but the ship was wrecked. It was stuck on the rocks and there

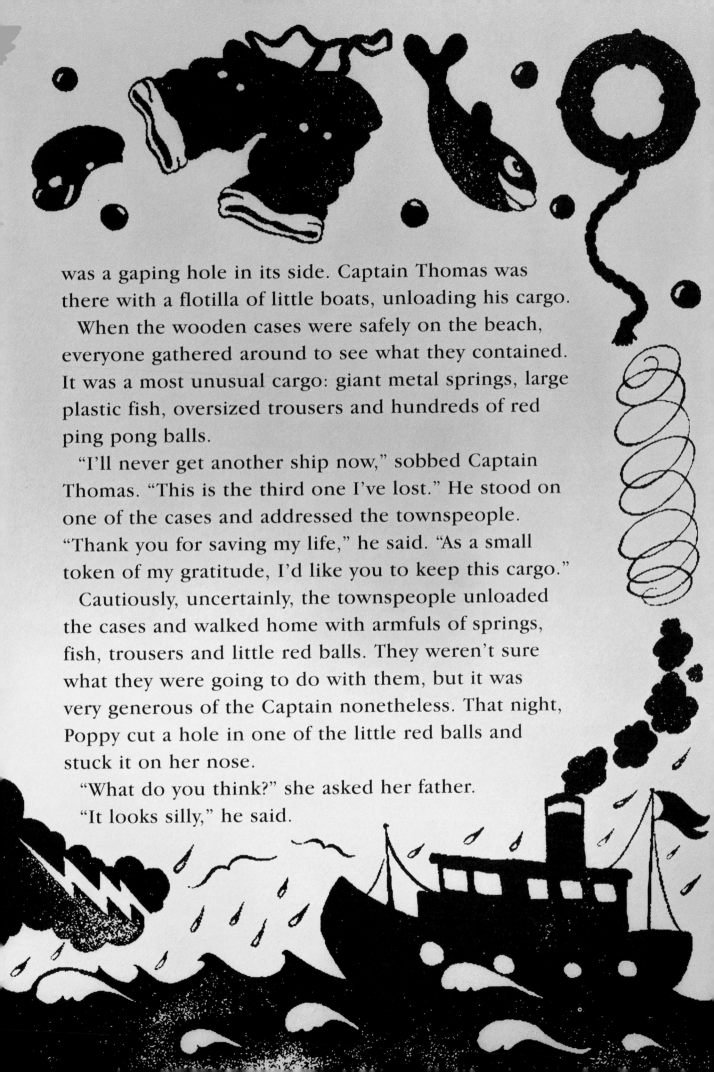

was a gaping hole in its side. Captain Thomas was there with a flotilla of little boats, unloading his cargo.

When the wooden cases were safely on the beach, everyone gathered around to see what they contained. It was a most unusual cargo: giant metal springs, large plastic fish, oversized trousers and hundreds of red ping pong balls.

"I'll never get another ship now," sobbed Captain Thomas. "This is the third one I've lost." He stood on one of the cases and addressed the townspeople. "Thank you for saving my life," he said. "As a small token of my gratitude, I'd like you to keep this cargo."

Cautiously, uncertainly, the townspeople unloaded the cases and walked home with armfuls of springs, fish, trousers and little red balls. They weren't sure what they were going to do with them, but it was very generous of the Captain nonetheless. That night, Poppy cut a hole in one of the little red balls and stuck it on her nose.

"What do you think?" she asked her father.

"It looks silly," he said.

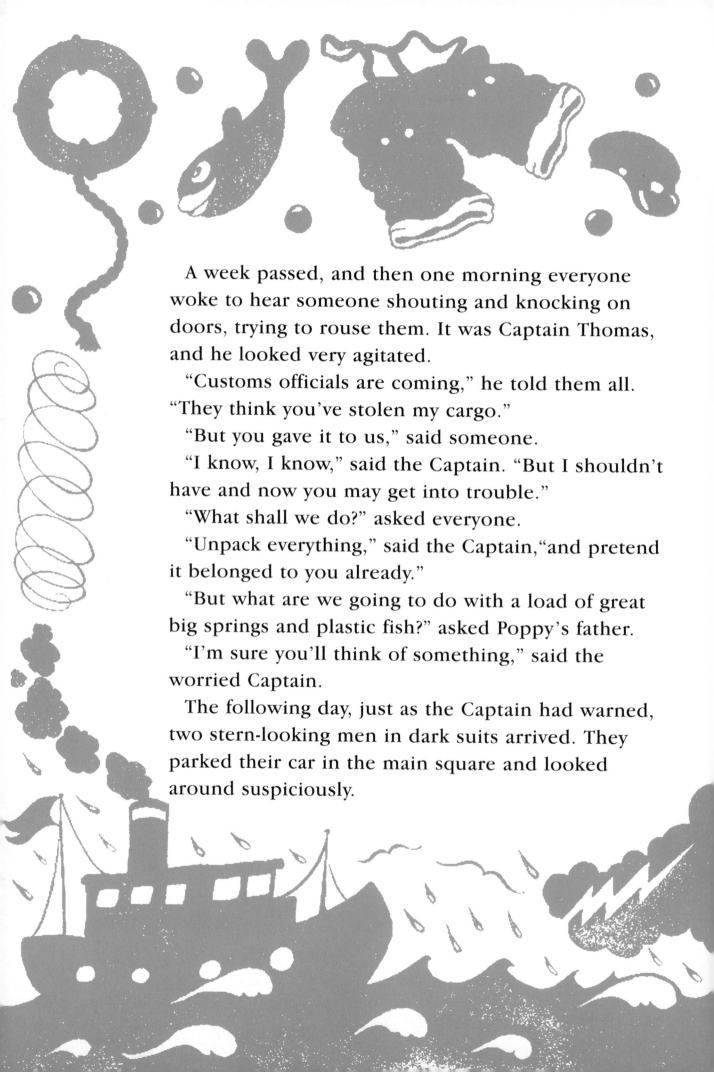

A week passed, and then one morning everyone woke to hear someone shouting and knocking on doors, trying to rouse them. It was Captain Thomas, and he looked very agitated.

"Customs officials are coming," he told them all. "They think you've stolen my cargo."

"But you gave it to us," said someone.

"I know, I know," said the Captain. "But I shouldn't have and now you may get into trouble."

"What shall we do?" asked everyone.

"Unpack everything," said the Captain, "and pretend it belonged to you already."

"But what are we going to do with a load of great big springs and plastic fish?" asked Poppy's father.

"I'm sure you'll think of something," said the worried Captain.

The following day, just as the Captain had warned, two stern-looking men in dark suits arrived. They parked their car in the main square and looked around suspiciously.

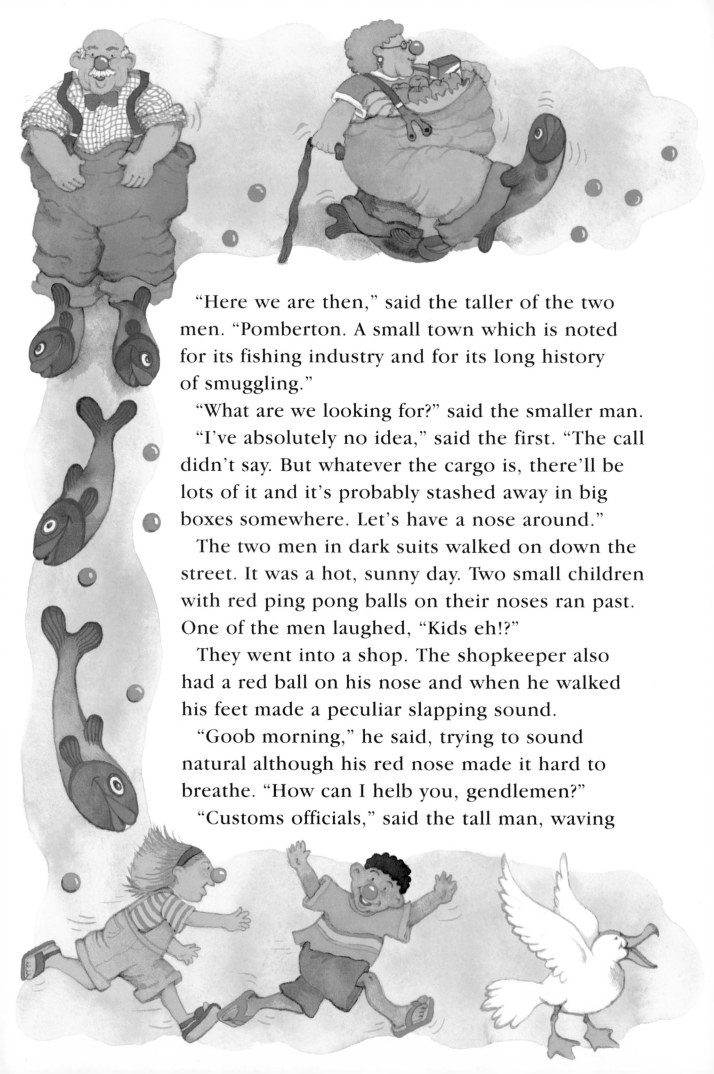

"Here we are then," said the taller of the two men. "Pomberton. A small town which is noted for its fishing industry and for its long history of smuggling."

"What are we looking for?" said the smaller man.

"I've absolutely no idea," said the first. "The call didn't say. But whatever the cargo is, there'll be lots of it and it's probably stashed away in big boxes somewhere. Let's have a nose around."

The two men in dark suits walked on down the street. It was a hot, sunny day. Two small children with red ping pong balls on their noses ran past. One of the men laughed, "Kids eh!?"

They went into a shop. The shopkeeper also had a red ball on his nose and when he walked his feet made a peculiar slapping sound.

"Goob morning," he said, trying to sound natural although his red nose made it hard to breathe. "How can I helb you, gendlemen?"

"Customs officials," said the tall man, waving

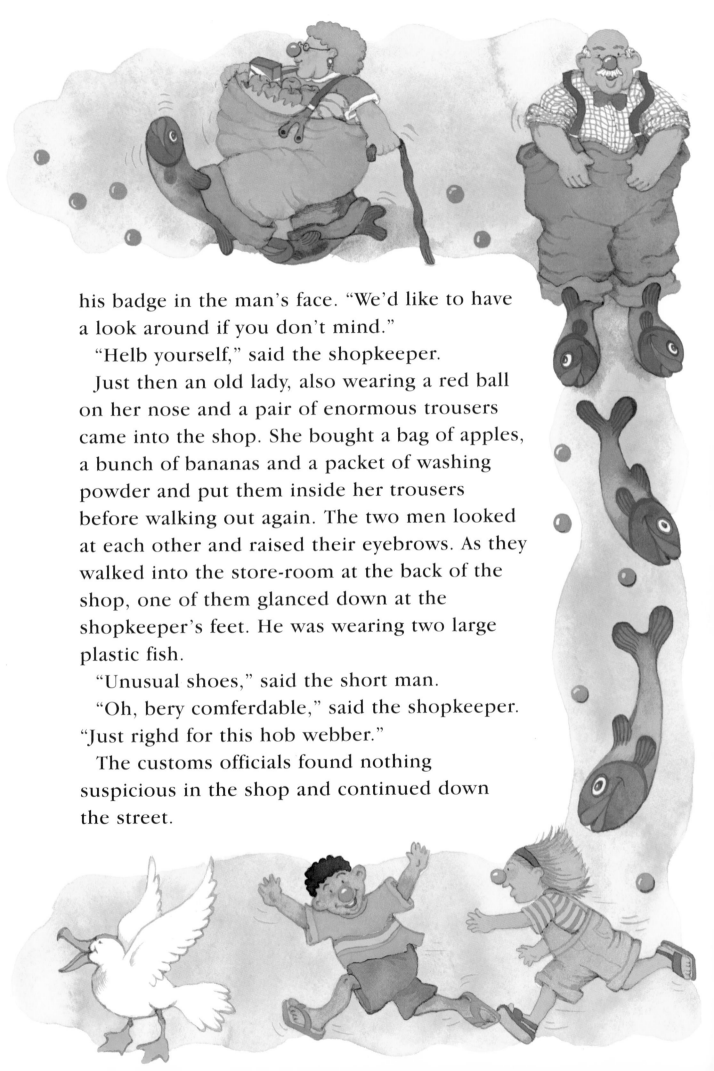

his badge in the man's face. "We'd like to have a look around if you don't mind."

"Helb yourself," said the shopkeeper.

Just then an old lady, also wearing a red ball on her nose and a pair of enormous trousers came into the shop. She bought a bag of apples, a bunch of bananas and a packet of washing powder and put them inside her trousers before walking out again. The two men looked at each other and raised their eyebrows. As they walked into the store-room at the back of the shop, one of them glanced down at the shopkeeper's feet. He was wearing two large plastic fish.

"Unusual shoes," said the short man.

"Oh, bery comferdable," said the shopkeeper. "Just righd for this hob webber."

The customs officials found nothing suspicious in the shop and continued down the street.

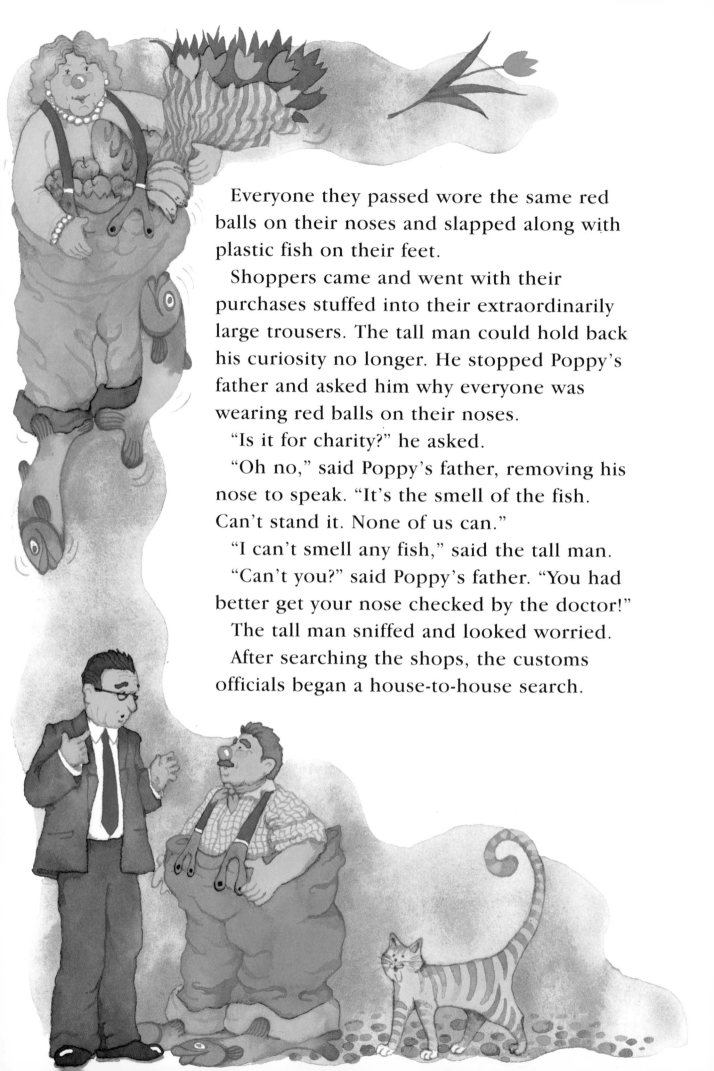

Everyone they passed wore the same red balls on their noses and slapped along with plastic fish on their feet.

Shoppers came and went with their purchases stuffed into their extraordinarily large trousers. The tall man could hold back his curiosity no longer. He stopped Poppy's father and asked him why everyone was wearing red balls on their noses.

"Is it for charity?" he asked.

"Oh no," said Poppy's father, removing his nose to speak. "It's the smell of the fish. Can't stand it. None of us can."

"I can't smell any fish," said the tall man.

"Can't you?" said Poppy's father. "You had better get your nose checked by the doctor!"

The tall man sniffed and looked worried.

After searching the shops, the customs officials began a house-to-house search.

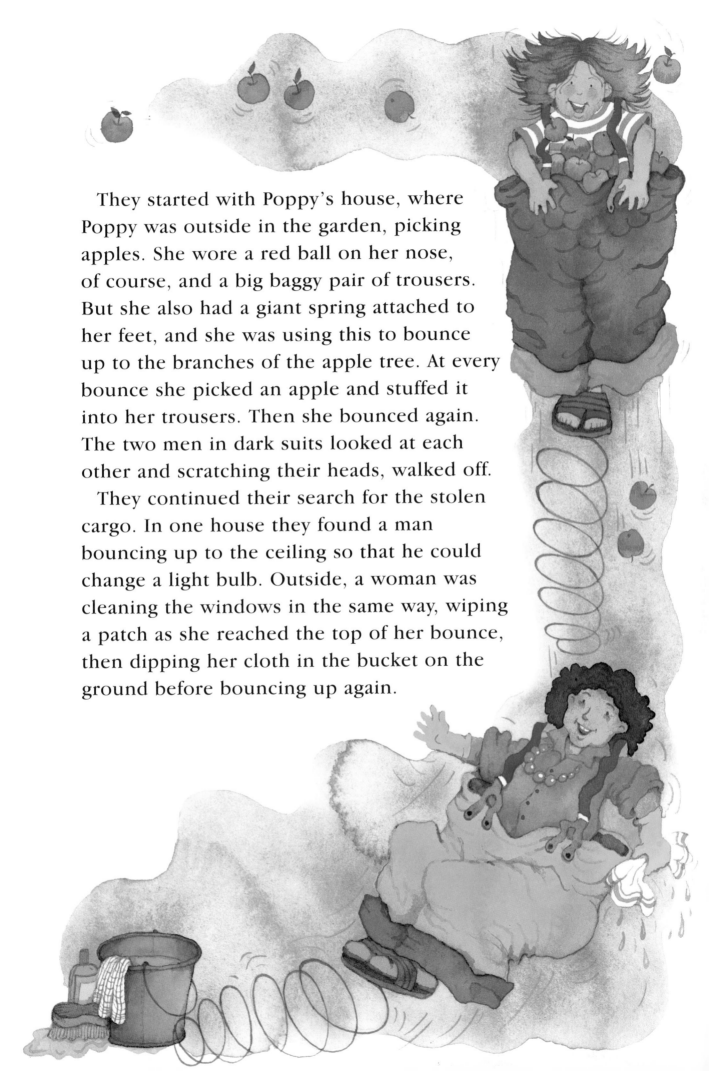

They started with Poppy's house, where Poppy was outside in the garden, picking apples. She wore a red ball on her nose, of course, and a big baggy pair of trousers. But she also had a giant spring attached to her feet, and she was using this to bounce up to the branches of the apple tree. At every bounce she picked an apple and stuffed it into her trousers. Then she bounced again. The two men in dark suits looked at each other and scratching their heads, walked off.

They continued their search for the stolen cargo. In one house they found a man bouncing up to the ceiling so that he could change a light bulb. Outside, a woman was cleaning the windows in the same way, wiping a patch as she reached the top of her bounce, then dipping her cloth in the bucket on the ground before bouncing up again.

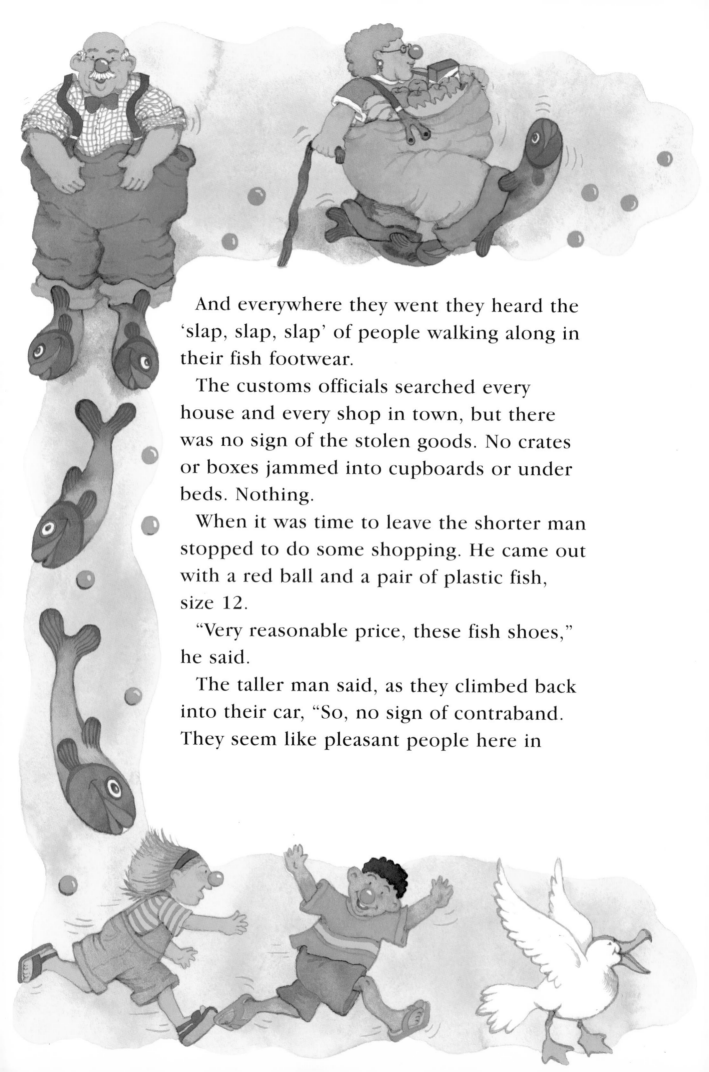

And everywhere they went they heard the 'slap, slap, slap' of people walking along in their fish footwear.

The customs officials searched every house and every shop in town, but there was no sign of the stolen goods. No crates or boxes jammed into cupboards or under beds. Nothing.

When it was time to leave the shorter man stopped to do some shopping. He came out with a red ball and a pair of plastic fish, size 12.

"Very reasonable price, these fish shoes," he said.

The taller man said, as they climbed back into their car, "So, no sign of contraband. They seem like pleasant people here in

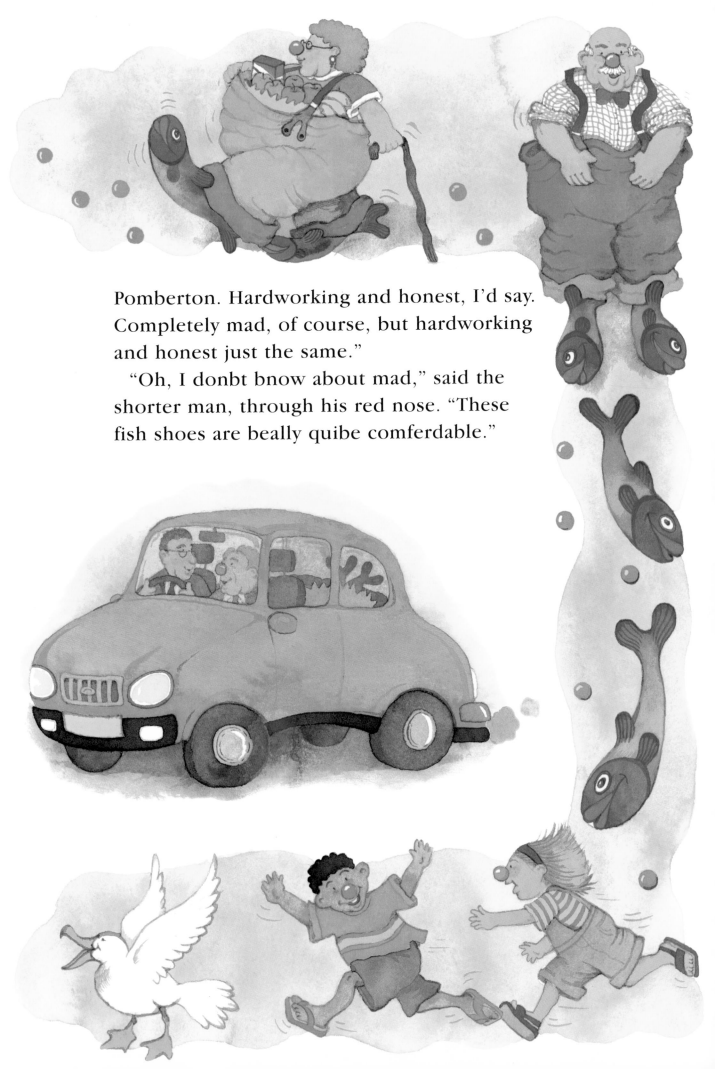

Pomberton. Hardworking and honest, I'd say. Completely mad, of course, but hardworking and honest just the same."

"Oh, I donbt bnow about mad," said the shorter man, through his red nose. "These fish shoes are beally quibe comferdable."

Cooking Up a Storm

I'm a wizard in the kitchen,
Or so my friends all say,
Just wait till they discover what
I'm cooking up today!

I've got my biggest cauldron
Heating up on the fire,
And I've gathered the ingredients
This fine spell will require!

First a handful of cat's whiskers,
The tails from three young pups,
A big ladle full of eyeballs,
And froggy slime– two cups!

Add a ton of giant fireworks,
A bunch of old tin cans,
A pair of cymbals, a big bass drum—
All stirred with a frying pan.

Bangs and crashes shake the windows,
It's raining cats and dogs,
Outside the storm is stirring up
A nasty shower of frogs!

For, although it may be August,
So sunny, bright and warm,
You'd better run for cover—
I've cooked up the perfect storm!

King Pong

There once lived a king who was very fond of
gardening. The royal garden was the talk of
the kingdom, and the king spent most of his
time tending the royal blooms. They were the most
magnificent flowers you could ever imagine.
There were vibrant violets, delicate delphiniums,
marvellous marigolds and even lovely ruby red
roses. The king could grow just about anything,
and everyone said that he had green fingers, but
this was largely due to the fact that he never
washed his hands.

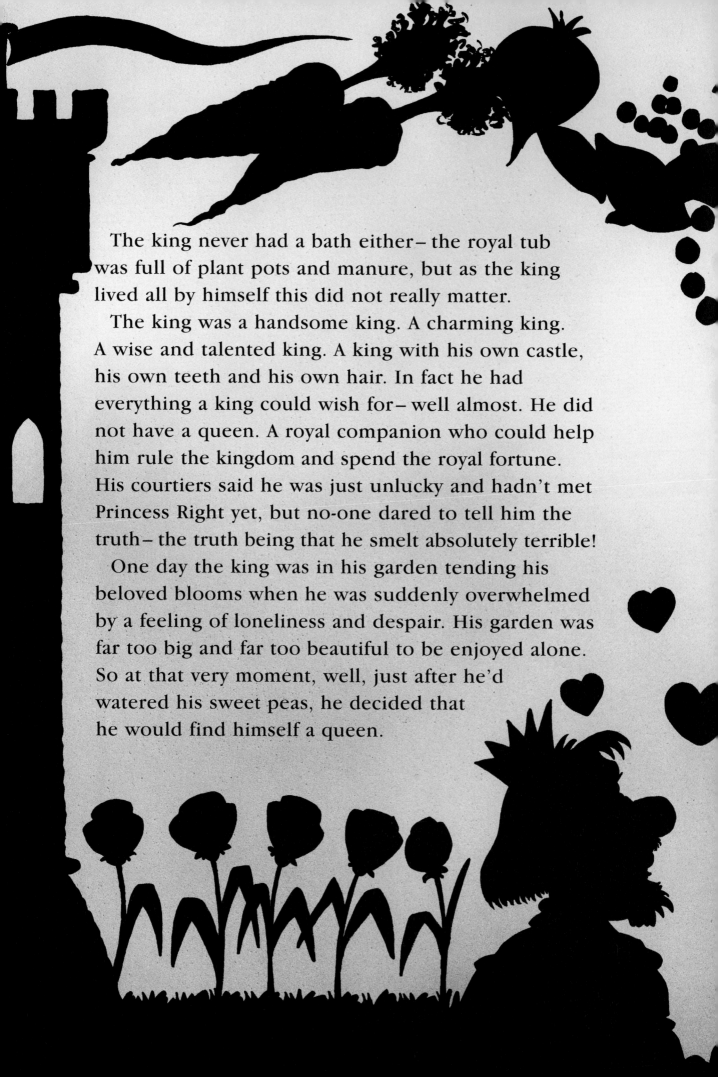

The king never had a bath either – the royal tub
was full of plant pots and manure, but as the king
lived all by himself this did not really matter.

The king was a handsome king. A charming king.
A wise and talented king. A king with his own castle,
his own teeth and his own hair. In fact he had
everything a king could wish for – well almost. He did
not have a queen. A royal companion who could help
him rule the kingdom and spend the royal fortune.
His courtiers said he was just unlucky and hadn't met
Princess Right yet, but no-one dared to tell him the
truth – the truth being that he smelt absolutely terrible!

One day the king was in his garden tending his
beloved blooms when he was suddenly overwhelmed
by a feeling of loneliness and despair. His garden was
far too big and far too beautiful to be enjoyed alone.
So at that very moment, well, just after he'd
watered his sweet peas, he decided that
he would find himself a queen.

That very afternoon the king took the royal rose
pruners and snipped and snipped until he had
a basket filled to the brim with glorious ruby red
roses. He then ordered a single red rose to be
sent to every eligible princess in the kingdom.
Each magnificent rose was to be accompanied
by a gold-edged invitation requesting the pleasure
of the company of the princess in question.
The roses and the invitations were duly despatched
and the king retired to his potting shed to wait.

But alas, although the rich velvety petals and
sweet scent of the roses enticed each princess to
make the journey to the king's castle, none were
able to travel further than the front gate, so
appalling was the smell that wafted towards their
delicate regal nostrils.

The king was about to give up hope of ever finding
a queen when, one day, a small neatly wrapped
parcel arrived with the royal breakfast tray.

Inside was a tiny bottle of vibrant orange liquid and a short hand written note, which read:

Her Royal Highness regrets that she is unable to accept your invitation, but thanks you for the delightful rose, which did incidentally have a touch of greenfly. Her Royal Highness has therefore taken the liberty of enclosing an excellent preparation which should combat this.

The king was intrigued. The very next day he ordered that one dozen royal red roses, minus green fly, of course, be despatched directly to the princess with another invitation asking if she would join him for afternoon tea on Tuesday at four o'clock prompt.

The next morning the king received a large, neatly wrapped parcel containing a splendid Savoy cabbage and a short hand written note which read:

Her Royal Highness thanks you most sincerely for the generous bouquet and trusts that you will accept this cabbage as a token of her appreciation. Sadly she is unable to accept your offer of tea.

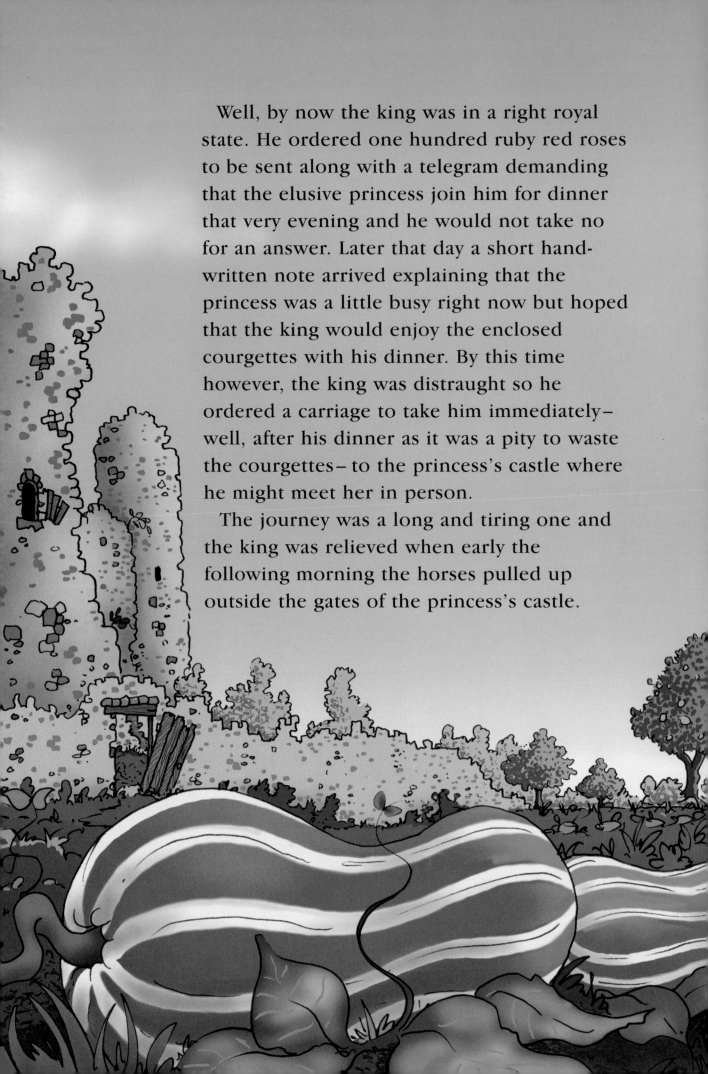

Well, by now the king was in a right royal state. He ordered one hundred ruby red roses to be sent along with a telegram demanding that the elusive princess join him for dinner that very evening and he would not take no for an answer. Later that day a short hand-written note arrived explaining that the princess was a little busy right now but hoped that the king would enjoy the enclosed courgettes with his dinner. By this time however, the king was distraught so he ordered a carriage to take him immediately–well, after his dinner as it was a pity to waste the courgettes– to the princess's castle where he might meet her in person.

The journey was a long and tiring one and the king was relieved when early the following morning the horses pulled up outside the gates of the princess's castle.

The king clambered out and gazed at the crumbling towers that held the crumbling walls of the castle together. It was very very run down. The gates were rusty and one was hanging off its hinges. Unperturbed the king walked up the uneven muddy driveway and knocked at the rotten front door of the castle. There was no reply, so he knocked again and he would have knocked a third time but the knocker came off in his hand so he decided to try round the back instead. He passed through a rickety wooden door set in an ancient moss-covered wall and found himself in the most fantastic vegetable garden he had ever seen.

There were marrows bigger than carriages, great fat pea pods ready to burst, cabbages, cauliflowers and lettuces all growing in perfectly straight lines and in such abundance it took your breath away.

At the far end of the garden he saw a figure effortlessly pulling up bunches of enormous juicy carrots and throwing them into the basket by her side. She was tall and very strong. Her hair was the colour of the carrots and hung in unruly curls about her grubby face. Her patched trousers were held up with string. She paused to wipe her nose on her sleeve and it was love at first sight. The king gave a little cough to attract her attention. The vision of loveliness looked up and the king walked steadily over to her, not noticing that she didn't smell particularly nice. He bowed politely and kissed her grimy hand. The princess blushed the colour of the wonderful beetroots that were sitting in her basket.

"I'm so glad you came," she said, offering him a radish. "It's been lonely since the staff left."

"You're very beautiful," the king told her and he meant it. The princess smiled a shy smile. "Oh you're just being nice," she said. "I'm afraid I've been so wrapped up in the garden I've rather neglected myself."

"Nonsense," said the king. "You are by far the prettiest flower in your garden."

"You are very kind," said the princess – who was far too polite to point out that she only grew vegetables.

The king then knelt in the slimy green mud to propose. Princess Composta, for that was her name, accepted without hesitation.

"We must be married at once," announced the king, and so they were – well, after he'd helped her dig up the spuds.

And they both lived smellily ever after.

Daft and Dafter

"Miaow!"
Tommy looked up at the faint sound of a kitten purring somewhere above his head. Then he blinked in amazement. The kitten was not stuck in a tree – it appeared to be floating down through the sky! Even more incredibly, other kittens were gently falling downwards. It couldn't be true! Were his eyes playing tricks? He looked up again. But it was true! And there were puppies floating down, as well!

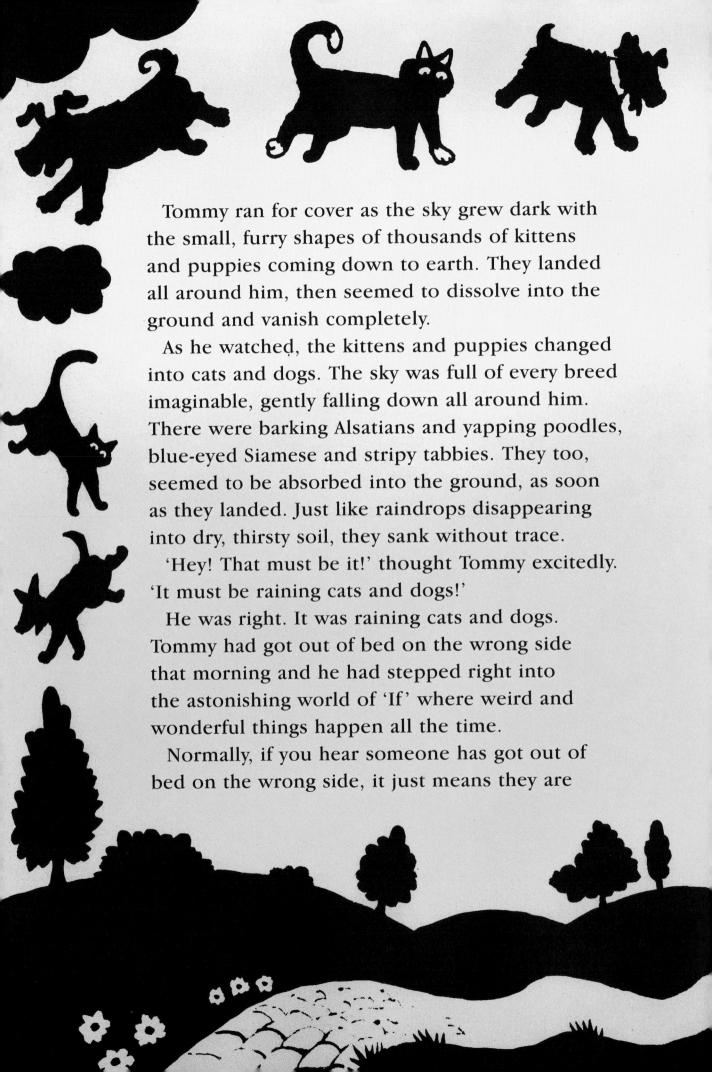

Tommy ran for cover as the sky grew dark with the small, furry shapes of thousands of kittens and puppies coming down to earth. They landed all around him, then seemed to dissolve into the ground and vanish completely.

As he watched, the kittens and puppies changed into cats and dogs. The sky was full of every breed imaginable, gently falling down all around him. There were barking Alsatians and yapping poodles, blue-eyed Siamese and stripy tabbies. They too, seemed to be absorbed into the ground, as soon as they landed. Just like raindrops disappearing into dry, thirsty soil, they sank without trace.

'Hey! That must be it!' thought Tommy excitedly. 'It must be raining cats and dogs!'

He was right. It was raining cats and dogs. Tommy had got out of bed on the wrong side that morning and he had stepped right into the astonishing world of 'If' where weird and wonderful things happen all the time.

Normally, if you hear someone has got out of bed on the wrong side, it just means they are very cross. But Tommy was not cross about it at all. On the contrary, he was delighted.

"Wow!" gasped Tommy, as the last dogs and cats vanished into the ground and the sun came out again. "What's going to happen next?"

He was standing in the middle of nowhere but there was a dazzling gold yellow-brick road beneath his feet. He decided to follow it. Maybe it was the same one that led to the Wizard of Oz, in that story he enjoyed so much?

But before he knew it – although because it was a magic road, it could have been hundreds of miles – he had reached the end. And it had stopped just outside a town quite unlike any other Tommy had ever seen.

Every single bit of it was painted the same shade of dazzling red. Its appearance made Tommy think of something his mother had once said to him about a friend of hers, who went out one night determined to have lots of fun.

"She really painted the town red," Tommy's mother had laughed when she told him about it.

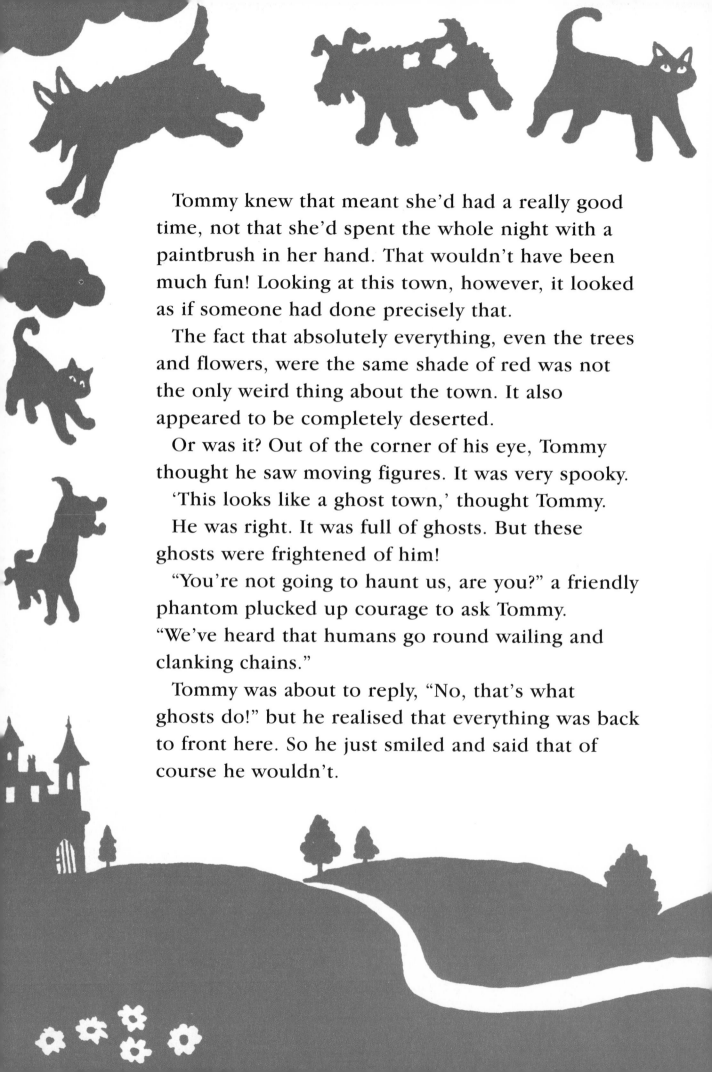

Tommy knew that meant she'd had a really good time, not that she'd spent the whole night with a paintbrush in her hand. That wouldn't have been much fun! Looking at this town, however, it looked as if someone had done precisely that.

The fact that absolutely everything, even the trees and flowers, were the same shade of red was not the only weird thing about the town. It also appeared to be completely deserted.

Or was it? Out of the corner of his eye, Tommy thought he saw moving figures. It was very spooky.

'This looks like a ghost town,' thought Tommy.

He was right. It was full of ghosts. But these ghosts were frightened of him!

"You're not going to haunt us, are you?" a friendly phantom plucked up courage to ask Tommy. "We've heard that humans go round wailing and clanking chains."

Tommy was about to reply, "No, that's what ghosts do!" but he realised that everything was back to front here. So he just smiled and said that of course he wouldn't.

However, Tommy was feeling a bit nervous himself and he was keen to explore the strange new world.

"I'm tired of seeing red," he told the phantom. "It's driving me up the wall."

His words came true. A moment later, Tommy found himself standing on the top of a great wall that went all around the town.

"I've been told that walls have ears," Tommy told it, jokingly. "Maybe you do! You are quite unlike any wall I've ever met."

"You needn't shout!" the wall retorted, proving that it did have excellent hearing.

Just then, a loud and very unexpected 'oink' sounded above Tommy's head, followed by a succession of noisy grunts. Tommy looked up and was amazed to see a herd of pigs flying towards him. They had made a V-shaped formation, like geese, but squealed rather than honked as they flew, propelling themselves along by flapping their huge pink ears.

"Well, if it can rain cats and dogs, there's no reason why pigs shouldn't fly!" Tommy laughed. "Maybe we could even hitch a ride on the back of one."

"Come on!" he shouted to the friendly ghost.

They both rose to the occasion– in the wonderful world of 'If', you really can– and floated upwards to join the flying pigs.

"You want to go the whole hog, do you?" squealed a large black-and-white sow with ten spotted piglets fluttering along behind her. "Well, jump aboard."

She flew them down to a beach and then took off again.

"I must keep up with the others," she grunted. "Or they'll have my bacon."

Tommy and the ghost made for the inviting blue sea. Curiously, it seemed to be singing. As Tommy got closer, he realised it was the sound of many different singsong voices, all talking at once but very softly. He couldn't hear what they were saying to him, but it all sounded very flattering.

"I think they must be whispering sweet nothings to me," Tommy laughed.

"Whhoo-oo, I love sweet nothings!" the ghost moaned with pleasure. "I'll sit here for a bit and fish for compliments."

He produced a fishing net out of thin air and dipped it into the ocean. But all he got for his pains, was a sackful of trouble.

This being 'If', however, it was not an imaginary sack full of imaginary troubles, it was the real thing.

"We're in for the high jump now,"
Tommy said anxiously, fearing the worst,
as the bulging bag was lifted out, dripping
with water and looking like a real load of
problems. He suddenly felt himself going
up in the world again. But this time it
was as if he was bouncing off an extra
springy trampoline.

"We're not 'in for the high jump', we are
in a high jump," Tommy called to the
phantom delightedly.

But when he finally came down to earth
again with a bump, there was no sign of
the friendly ghost. In fact, he was right
back where he had started – in bed.

And Tommy did wonder if he might not
have dreamed the whole thing. Just in case,
he quickly looked out of the window to see
if it was still raining cats and dogs – but
there was only a clear blue sky!

When Dreams Come True

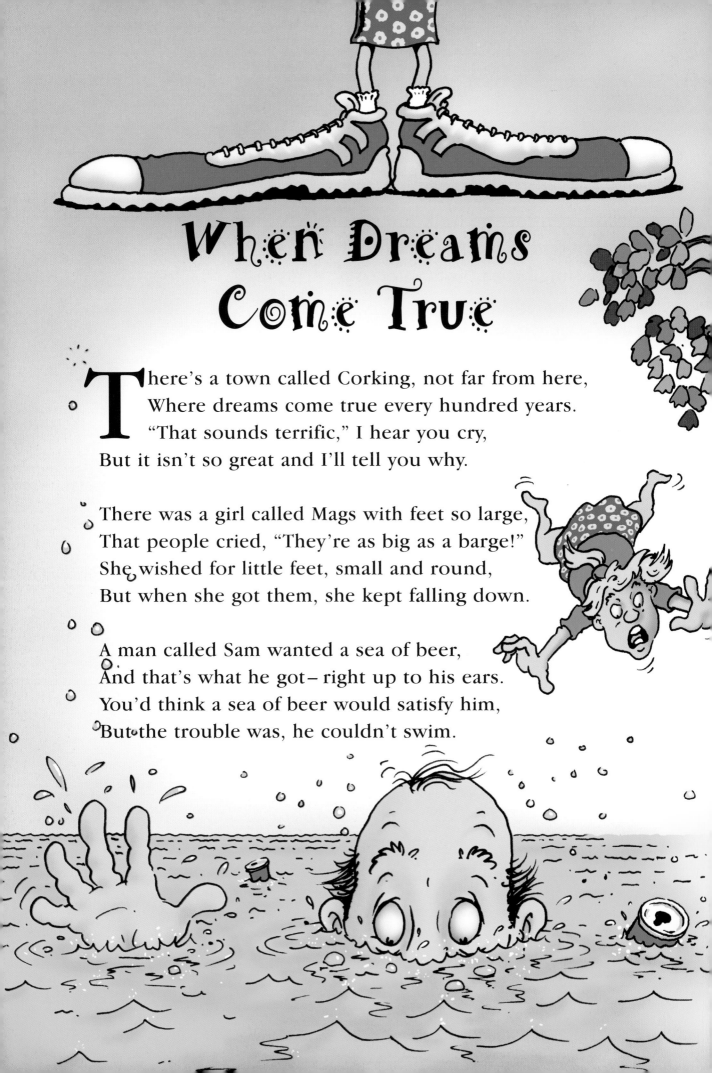

There's a town called Corking, not far from here,
Where dreams come true every hundred years.
"That sounds terrific," I hear you cry,
But it isn't so great and I'll tell you why.

There was a girl called Mags with feet so large,
That people cried, "They're as big as a barge!"
She wished for little feet, small and round,
But when she got them, she kept falling down.

A man called Sam wanted a sea of beer,
And that's what he got– right up to his ears.
You'd think a sea of beer would satisfy him,
But the trouble was, he couldn't swim.

There was a girl called Lucy who climbed into trees,
Because she wanted to talk to the birds and bees,
But the sparrows and starlings all wanted a word,
And poor little Lucy couldn't make herself heard.

There was a boy called Arnie who wished he was strong.
His dream came true, but it didn't last long.
Everything he touched just snapped into two,
And in no time at all, he had run out of glue.

So you see what I'm getting at in this little rhyme,
It's easy to work out, if you give it some time.
Beware what you wish for – and I'm talking to you,
You never know, it might come true!

Follow the Leader

Sasha the sheep lived, as most sheep do, in a large field with a whole bunch of other sheep, carefully watched over by the farmer and his trusty sheepdogs. The farmer seemed to be a reasonable sort of chap, who made sure they had everything they needed, but the sheepdogs were a surly, miserable bunch, forever barking out their orders and expecting to be obeyed. This suited the other sheep quite well, as they were not good at thinking for themselves. But Sasha… well, Sasha was… different.

Ever since she was a tiny lamb her mother had known she would not grow up to be an ordinary sheep. While the other little lambs frolicked gaily in the meadow, chasing each other and gambolling nimbly, Sasha strode back and forth at the edge of the field, muttering fiercely under her breath. When she grew older she would sit for hours with her head buried in a book, or scribbling furiously on little pieces of paper which she hid in the bushes. Other times she went missing altogether, which sent her mother into a frenzy, convinced she had been carried off by a wolf. Then she would find her, propped upside down behind a tree. Meditating, Sasha called it. Getting in touch with her inner self. And it seemed that Sasha had an awful lot of self to get in touch with. The teenage years were the worst– she would stomp round the field, in one of her "moods," glowering at anyone who tried to follow her.

She dyed her wool purple, and brushed it up into stiff spikes. She even had a ring put in her nose. "Very unbecoming, dear," said her mother mildly. "Those are just for bulls!" But Sasha would hear none of it. "I am an artist," she would cry. "I must give vent to my creative urges and express my individuality!" What it all boiled down to was that Sasha simply wasn't happy just being one of the flock. She had a problem, and her problem was the other sheep. Sasha could not conceive of a more dull and unimaginative bunch! For no matter what she did to set herself apart, the other silly creatures were bound to copy her. And as she grew older, things grew worse. Quite unwillingly she became a trendsetter, a style guru, and whether it was having her wool sheared in stylish patterns, or sporting a feather boa and dark glasses, you can be sure that where she led, the others were sure to follow!

"It's the highest form of flattery, dear!" said her
mother. "Baloney!" said Sasha.

And so it was one morning that Sasha woke in
a particularly foul temper, having discovered all
the other sheep copying her latest 'pirate' look–
eyepatch and spotted headscarf– to find a
handsome new sheepdog standing over her.
"Get lost!" she growled, staring up at him.

"You must be Sasha," he smiled. "I've heard a
lot about you from the other dogs– none of it
good, mind you! I'm Sid. Do me a favour and
come and lead this daft lot into the next field,
will you? I want to make a good impression on
my first day!" Now, as a rule, Sasha never did
anything a dog asked her to. But there was
something about Sid that made her sit up and
take notice. He was different from the others.
Pleasant, for a start. And then she noticed that
his eyes were different colours– one blue,
one brown!

'How brilliantly individual,' thought Sasha. The fact he thought the other sheep daft was just the icing on the cake! Sasha was smitten! The farmer could hardly believe his eyes when he saw Sasha jump up and do exactly as Sid directed. She had always been so very difficult before. Well, well, well – perhaps she'd finally met her match!

Which, of course, is exactly what had happened, although not in the way the farmer was thinking. From then on Sasha and Sid were inseparable. In fact, the farmer was so impressed by their teamwork that he decided to enter them in the individual sheepdog trials at the forthcoming county show. Dutifully they practised their routine every day, with Sid lying low in the grass listening attentively to the farmer's low whistles, and directing Sasha in a series of intricate manoeuvres. They were

magnificent, moving together as one,
in perfect harmony. The farmer felt sure
they would take the county show by storm.
Little did he know that is just what they
were planning to do – but again, not in the
way the farmer was thinking! For every night,
once the others were asleep, Sasha and Sid
had been hard at work secretly practising a
special routine of their own!

Well, the day of the sheepdog trials finally
dawned, and there was great excitement as
the sheepdogs rounded up the sheep and
herded them, led of course by Sasha, into the
farmer's truck. At the show, they sat dutifully
in their pen, and watched team after team of
dogs and sheep go through their manoeuvres.

"Mind-numbingly dull, isn't it!" Sasha
muttered to Sid. "Have they no imagination
at all?"

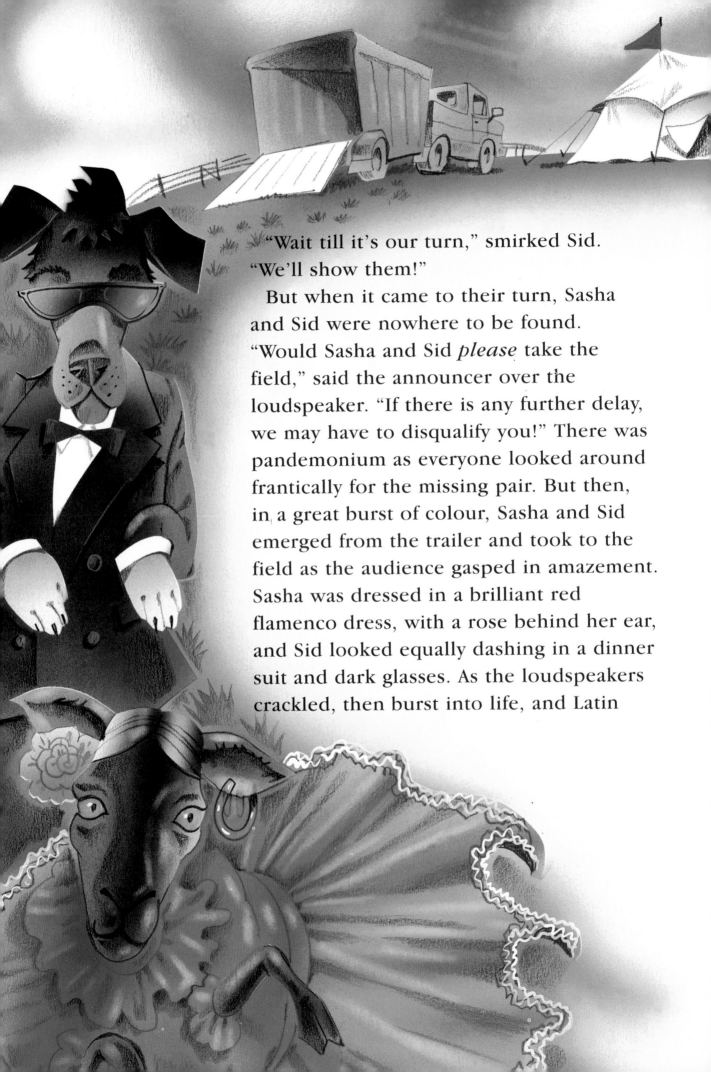

"Wait till it's our turn," smirked Sid. "We'll show them!"

But when it came to their turn, Sasha and Sid were nowhere to be found. "Would Sasha and Sid *please* take the field," said the announcer over the loudspeaker. "If there is any further delay, we may have to disqualify you!" There was pandemonium as everyone looked around frantically for the missing pair. But then, in a great burst of colour, Sasha and Sid emerged from the trailer and took to the field as the audience gasped in amazement. Sasha was dressed in a brilliant red flamenco dress, with a rose behind her ear, and Sid looked equally dashing in a dinner suit and dark glasses. As the loudspeakers crackled, then burst into life, and Latin music boomed across the field, Sasha and Sid sprang into action. They danced the samba, lambada and salsa, moving together in perfect harmony! The judges were outraged and disqualified them at once. Never had such a thing happened at their show! But Sasha and Sid just kept on dancing, as the crowd clapped and cheered, putting on a show no-one would ever forget, and securing Sasha's place in the history books as a sheep quite unlike any other! Even the farmer was pleased – after all, it was great publicity!

As she snuggled down to sleep next to Sid that night, Sasha felt truly happy. She had made her mark at last. Funnily enough though, salsa dancing has become awfully popular these days...

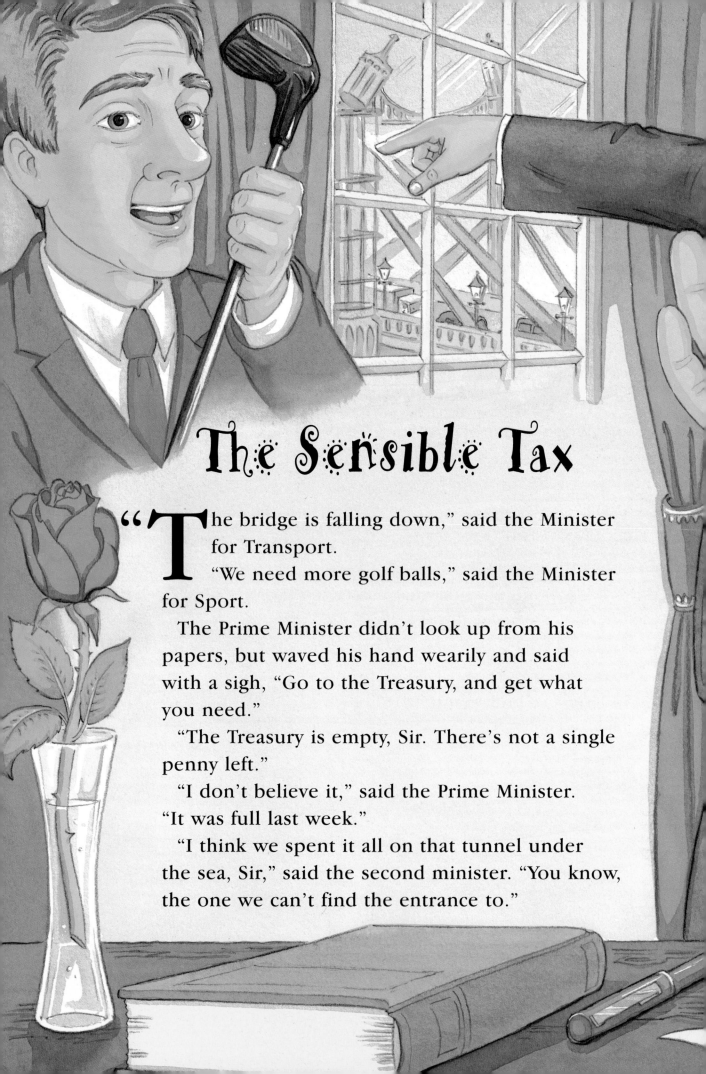

The Sensible Tax

"The bridge is falling down," said the Minister for Transport.

"We need more golf balls," said the Minister for Sport.

The Prime Minister didn't look up from his papers, but waved his hand wearily and said with a sigh, "Go to the Treasury, and get what you need."

"The Treasury is empty, Sir. There's not a single penny left."

"I don't believe it," said the Prime Minister. "It was full last week."

"I think we spent it all on that tunnel under the sea, Sir," said the second minister. "You know, the one we can't find the entrance to."

"Don't remind me!" said the Prime Minister.

Together, the three important gentlemen ran down to the Treasury. It was empty. Where once there were piles of gold and silver coins there was now nothing, just big balls of dust rolling across the bare floor.

The Prime Minister called a meeting.

"We need to come up with a new tax to raise some more money," he said. "What haven't we taxed yet?"

The ministers looked at him in silence.

"How about food?" said the Prime Minister.

"We've taxed that already," said someone.

"Roads?"

"Those too," said another.

"Windows? Pets? Water? Music? There must be something that the people do, or want, or can't help being that we could tax," said the Prime Minister.

One of his advisors coughed. "There is one thing," he said.

"Yes?" asked the Prime Minister.

"Well, we raise our children to be very sensible," said the man. "We teach them to wipe their feet when they enter the house, to

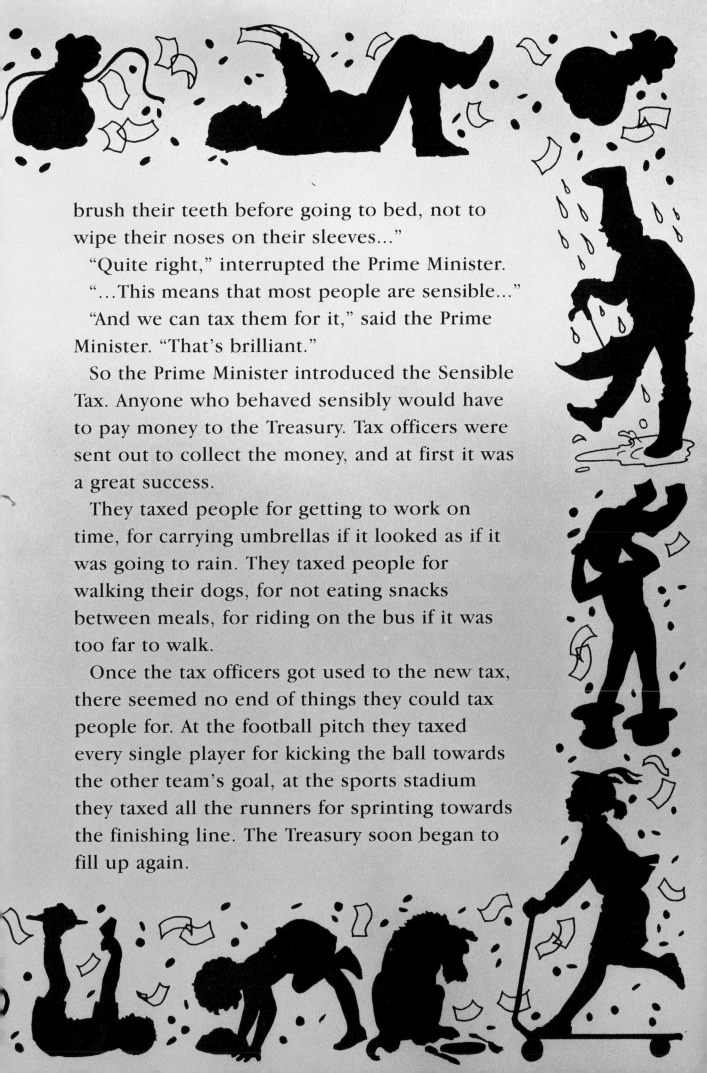

brush their teeth before going to bed, not to wipe their noses on their sleeves..."

"Quite right," interrupted the Prime Minister.

"...This means that most people are sensible..."

"And we can tax them for it," said the Prime Minister. "That's brilliant."

So the Prime Minister introduced the Sensible Tax. Anyone who behaved sensibly would have to pay money to the Treasury. Tax officers were sent out to collect the money, and at first it was a great success.

They taxed people for getting to work on time, for carrying umbrellas if it looked as if it was going to rain. They taxed people for walking their dogs, for not eating snacks between meals, for riding on the bus if it was too far to walk.

Once the tax officers got used to the new tax, there seemed no end of things they could tax people for. At the football pitch they taxed every single player for kicking the ball towards the other team's goal, at the sports stadium they taxed all the runners for sprinting towards the finishing line. The Treasury soon began to fill up again.

Of course, the new tax wasn't very popular with the people, and very soon they began to grumble.

"I've just been taxed for wearing my scarf," said Benjamin's dad when he came home from work one evening.

"Why were you wearing your scarf, George?" said his wife, Myrtle.

"Well, it's cold out," he asked.

"Yes, of course," she replied.

"This is ridiculous," said George. "All our lives we are told to be sensible and now they charge us for it. It's not a sensible tax, it's a completely stupid tax. The only people who never have to pay anything are those who are as daft as ducks."

Just then there was a knock at the door.

"I'm a tax officer," said the man at the door.

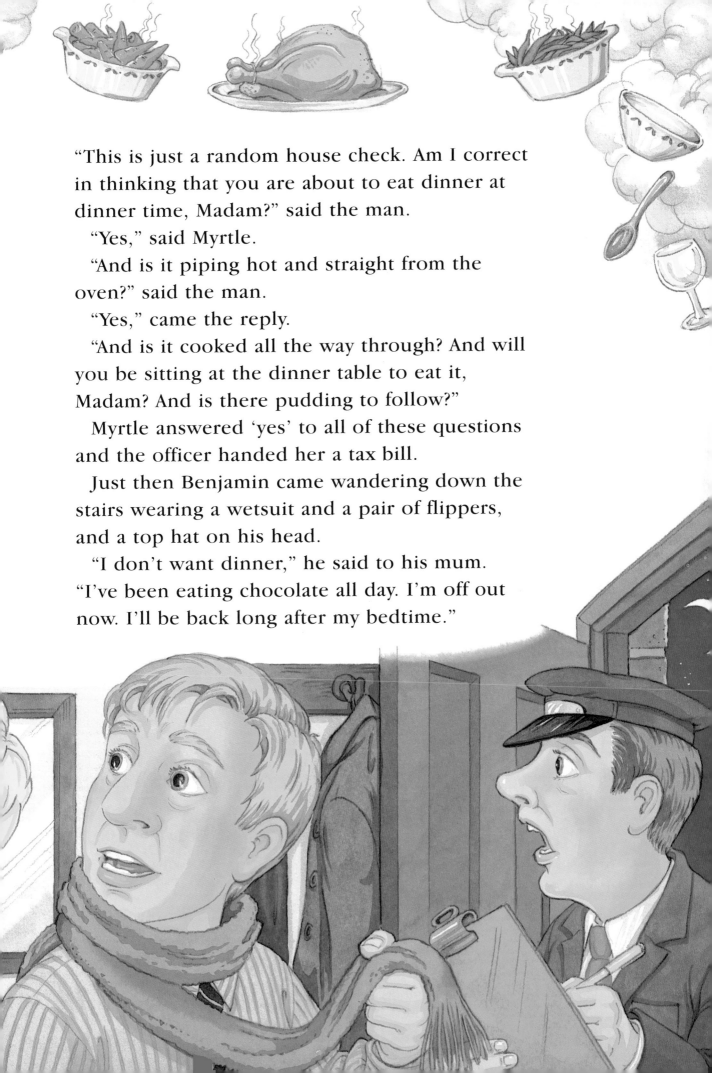

"This is just a random house check. Am I correct in thinking that you are about to eat dinner at dinner time, Madam?" said the man.

"Yes," said Myrtle.

"And is it piping hot and straight from the oven?" said the man.

"Yes," came the reply.

"And is it cooked all the way through? And will you be sitting at the dinner table to eat it, Madam? And is there pudding to follow?"

Myrtle answered 'yes' to all of these questions and the officer handed her a tax bill.

Just then Benjamin came wandering down the stairs wearing a wetsuit and a pair of flippers, and a top hat on his head.

"I don't want dinner," he said to his mum. "I've been eating chocolate all day. I'm off out now. I'll be back long after my bedtime."

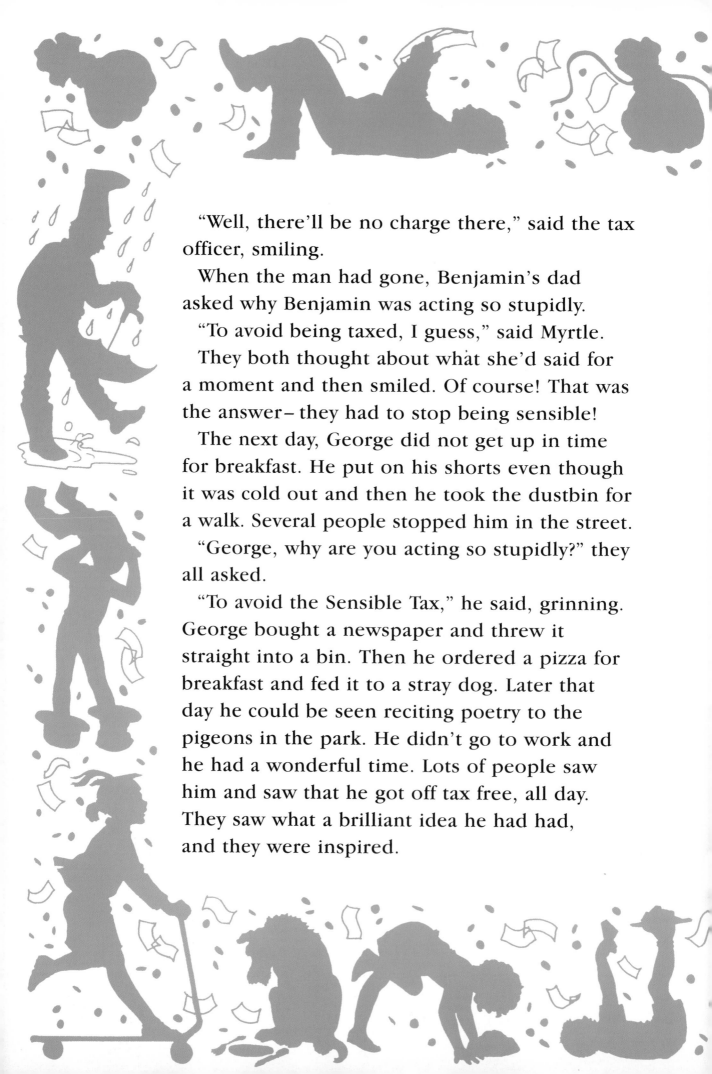

"Well, there'll be no charge there," said the tax officer, smiling.

When the man had gone, Benjamin's dad asked why Benjamin was acting so stupidly.

"To avoid being taxed, I guess," said Myrtle.

They both thought about what she'd said for a moment and then smiled. Of course! That was the answer– they had to stop being sensible!

The next day, George did not get up in time for breakfast. He put on his shorts even though it was cold out and then he took the dustbin for a walk. Several people stopped him in the street.

"George, why are you acting so stupidly?" they all asked.

"To avoid the Sensible Tax," he said, grinning. George bought a newspaper and threw it straight into a bin. Then he ordered a pizza for breakfast and fed it to a stray dog. Later that day he could be seen reciting poetry to the pigeons in the park. He didn't go to work and he had a wonderful time. Lots of people saw him and saw that he got off tax free, all day. They saw what a brilliant idea he had had, and they were inspired.

The next day, most people didn't go to work at all, and those who did didn't get there on time; some even went to the wrong jobs. They walked if it was too far to walk; if they had bicycles, they carried them. A lot of people went to the cinema in the afternoon dressed as pirates, but they didn't watch the film. No, that would have been too sensible. They faced the other way and sang football songs at the tops of their voices, instead.

They all had a great day, and the next day they all got up late and did it all over again, only this time they found even more ways to be silly.

The tax officers began to look worried – the money had stopped coming in – and the ministers were even more worried. No-one was doing any work; the country was falling apart. They called an emergency meeting with the Prime Minister.

"Sorry I'm late," said the Prime Minister. "My train didn't leave on time and then it went off in the wrong direction. It's chaos out there. What's going on?"

"It's the Sensible Tax, Sir," said one of his ministers. "Everyone is acting stupidly so that they don't have to pay it."

"Well, this can't go on," said the Prime Minister. "The country's gone mad."

"We shall have to stop the tax," someone said.

The Prime Minister paused. He liked the Sensible Tax; it raised lots of money. Without it the Treasury would be empty again. But things were getting out of hand.

"Yes," he said, sadly. And then he smiled. "I've got it," he cried. "Why don't we tax people for wearing clothes?"

All the ministers threw up their hands in complete despair.

"Oh no!" they groaned.

It's Raining

It's raining cats and dogs,
And warty toads and frogs,
And red-kneed bats and bowler hats.
It's raining big fat hogs.

It's raining needles and pins,
And rusty cans and tins,
And things I don't like – such as bits of bike.
It's raining wheelie bins.

It's raining sugar and spice,
And sleek white rats and mice,
And currant buns and somebody's sons.
It's raining furry dice.

It's raining apples and pears,
And dolls and teddy bears,
And silly pigs in curly wigs.
It's raining plastic chairs.

It's raining shoes and socks,
And pebbles, stones and rocks,
And kipper ties and old pork pies.
It's raining party frocks.

It's raining bacon and eggs,
And washing lines and pegs,
And cowboy suits and exotic fruits.
It's raining hairy legs.

It's raining ducks and drakes,
And chocolate bars and cakes,
And glasses of milk and colourful silk.
It's raining garden rakes.

The Underwater Talent Show

Every morning for the past week, Prawn had woken up in a panic. Today was no different. 'What day is it?' he thought, treading water so frantically that he spun round in circles until his spindly legs got tangled up. He realised with a sinking heart that it was Saturday– the day of the Talent Show.

Prawn had never felt so talentless. All week he had tried to devise amazing feats to dazzle the talent show judges. He tried to lift ten sea slugs with his bare antennae but he couldn't even lift one! When he tried to pick one up he was horribly stung by the outraged sea slug, who thought he was being very cheeky.

Then Prawn thought he'd try his hand at karaoke. A friendly DJ called Cool Daddy Squid mixed a tape of Prawn's favourite songs, to which they gave the title Prawn's Cocktail. The tape included such classic sounds as Shellfish Lover and Hake, Rattle and Roll. Prawn certainly looked the part as he grabbed the microphone, dressed in a spangled waistcoat and shades. The problem was his singing– or rather squeaking. The unfortunate truth was that Prawn had the most awful singing voice. A passing shoal of herring darted away in disgust and Hermit Crab moved deeper inside his shell and sealed the entrance fast, while Prawn screeched his way through the tunes.

"Enough!" bellowed Cool Daddy Squid, switching off the tape and ripping off his headphones. "I should try crochet instead," he added sarcastically as he swam away, leaving poor Prawn feeling quite miserable.

'Squid's right in a way,' thought Prawn, dejectedly. 'I'm a modest fellow. I should

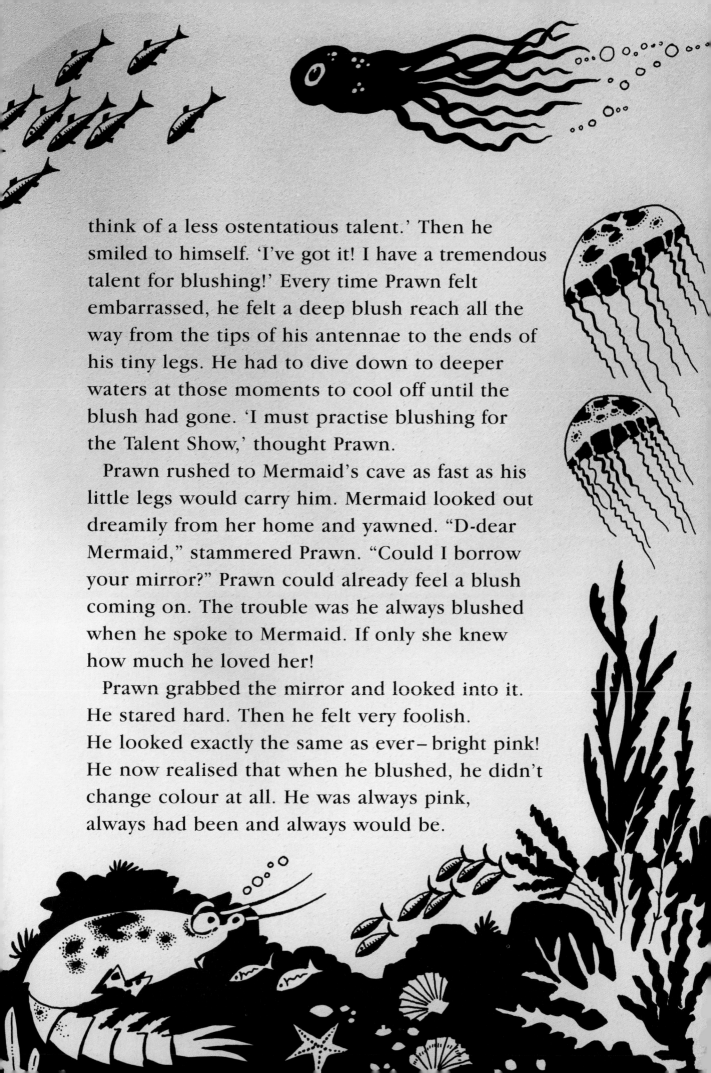

think of a less ostentatious talent.' Then he smiled to himself. 'I've got it! I have a tremendous talent for blushing!' Every time Prawn felt embarrassed, he felt a deep blush reach all the way from the tips of his antennae to the ends of his tiny legs. He had to dive down to deeper waters at those moments to cool off until the blush had gone. 'I must practise blushing for the Talent Show,' thought Prawn.

Prawn rushed to Mermaid's cave as fast as his little legs would carry him. Mermaid looked out dreamily from her home and yawned. "D-dear Mermaid," stammered Prawn. "Could I borrow your mirror?" Prawn could already feel a blush coming on. The trouble was he always blushed when he spoke to Mermaid. If only she knew how much he loved her!

Prawn grabbed the mirror and looked into it. He stared hard. Then he felt very foolish. He looked exactly the same as ever – bright pink! He now realised that when he blushed, he didn't change colour at all. He was always pink, always had been and always would be.

Mermaid gazed at Prawn from under her lovely lashes. "What's up, Prawn?" she drawled. "You look upset." "Oh, n-nothing," replied Prawn, as he handed her the mirror. She was looking at him with her clear, blue eyes and Prawn couldn't think of anything to say. "Must dash. Loads to do," he gulped as he paddled off. 'Ah, he is sweet,' thought Mermaid wistfully, as she went back into her cave.

Prawn was sad. The talent show would be starting soon, and he had nothing to offer. As Prawn peeped out through the weeds, he could see that the ocean was alive with excited and purposeful activity. A group of clams were practising opening and closing their shells in sequence. Anglerfish was unscrewing the light at the end of his fishing rod and changing it for a glitter ball. Then Prawn spotted Cool Daddy Squid with a nervous-looking young starfish at his side. "You're gonna be the greatest!" he heard Cool Daddy whisper to the starfish.

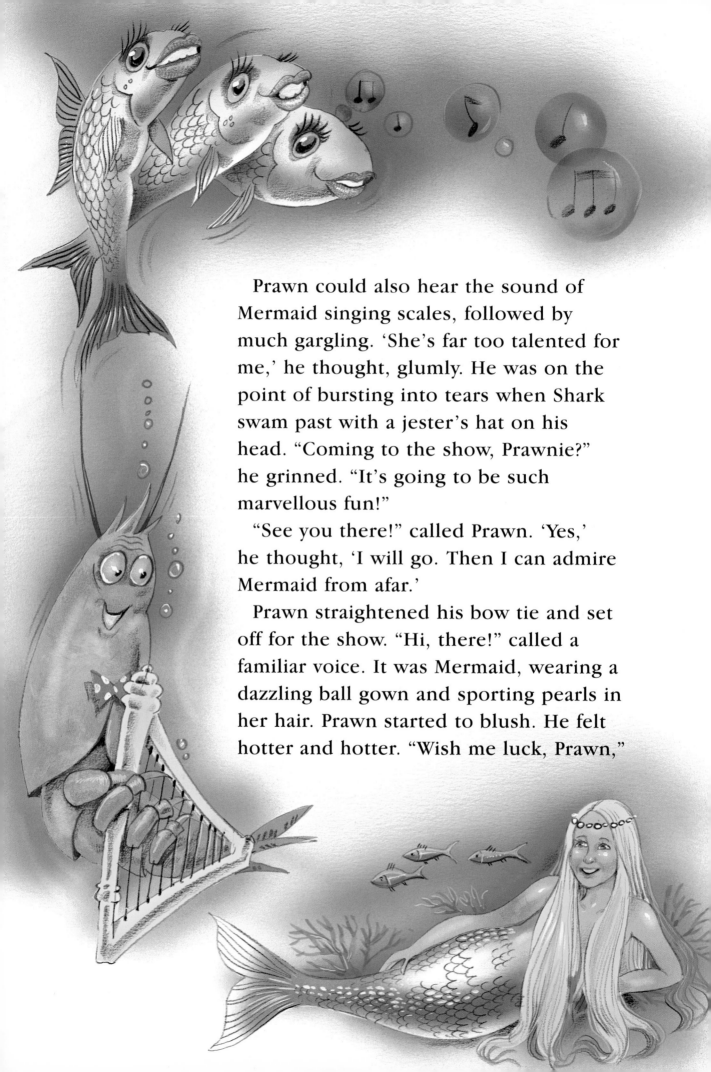

Prawn could also hear the sound of Mermaid singing scales, followed by much gargling. 'She's far too talented for me,' he thought, glumly. He was on the point of bursting into tears when Shark swam past with a jester's hat on his head. "Coming to the show, Prawnie?" he grinned. "It's going to be such marvellous fun!"

"See you there!" called Prawn. 'Yes,' he thought, 'I will go. Then I can admire Mermaid from afar.'

Prawn straightened his bow tie and set off for the show. "Hi, there!" called a familiar voice. It was Mermaid, wearing a dazzling ball gown and sporting pearls in her hair. Prawn started to blush. He felt hotter and hotter. "Wish me luck, Prawn,"

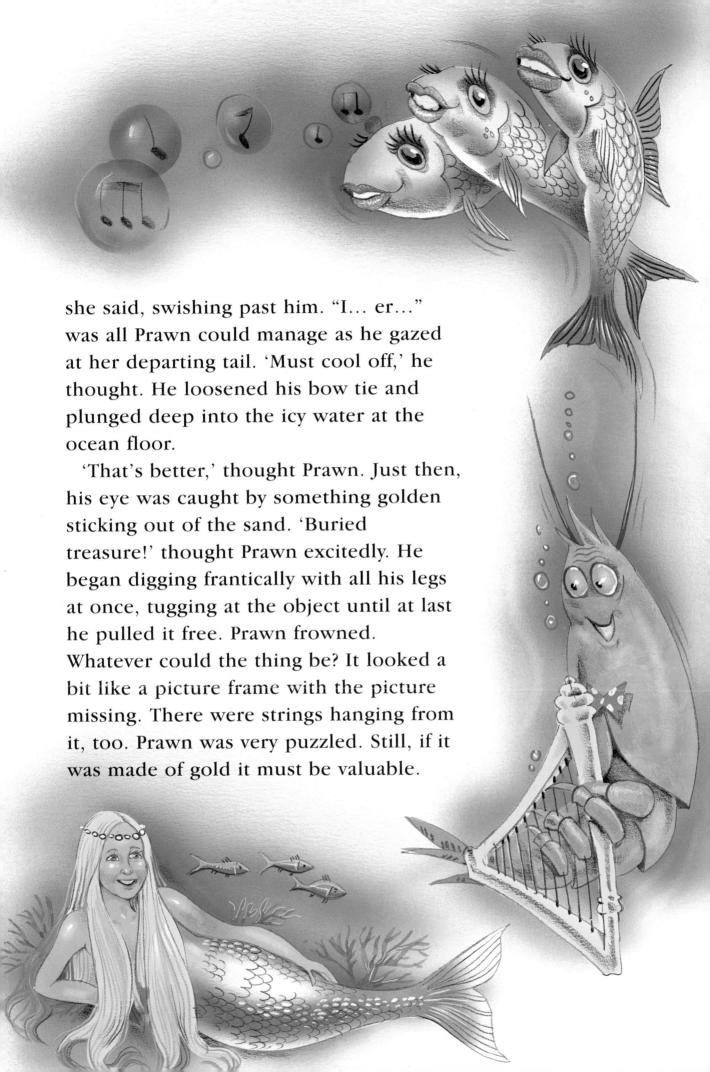

she said, swishing past him. "I... er..." was all Prawn could manage as he gazed at her departing tail. 'Must cool off,' he thought. He loosened his bow tie and plunged deep into the icy water at the ocean floor.

'That's better,' thought Prawn. Just then, his eye was caught by something golden sticking out of the sand. 'Buried treasure!' thought Prawn excitedly. He began digging frantically with all his legs at once, tugging at the object until at last he pulled it free. Prawn frowned. Whatever could the thing be? It looked a bit like a picture frame with the picture missing. There were strings hanging from it, too. Prawn was very puzzled. Still, if it was made of gold it must be valuable.

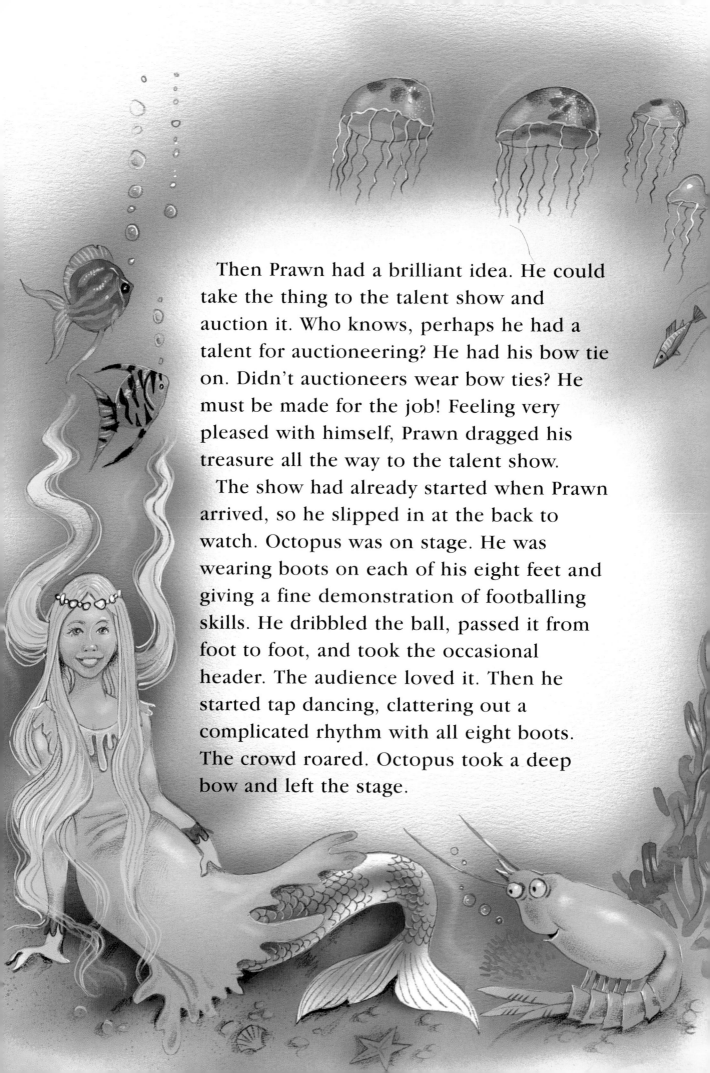

Then Prawn had a brilliant idea. He could take the thing to the talent show and auction it. Who knows, perhaps he had a talent for auctioneering? He had his bow tie on. Didn't auctioneers wear bow ties? He must be made for the job! Feeling very pleased with himself, Prawn dragged his treasure all the way to the talent show.

The show had already started when Prawn arrived, so he slipped in at the back to watch. Octopus was on stage. He was wearing boots on each of his eight feet and giving a fine demonstration of footballing skills. He dribbled the ball, passed it from foot to foot, and took the occasional header. The audience loved it. Then he started tap dancing, clattering out a complicated rhythm with all eight boots. The crowd roared. Octopus took a deep bow and left the stage.

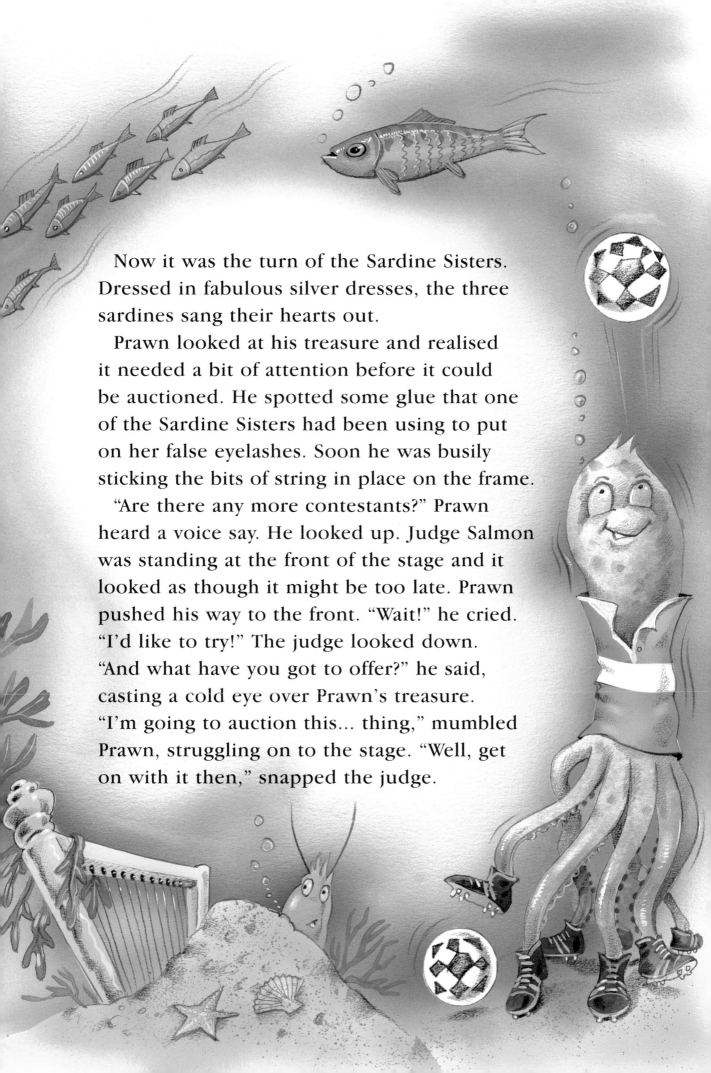

Now it was the turn of the Sardine Sisters. Dressed in fabulous silver dresses, the three sardines sang their hearts out.

Prawn looked at his treasure and realised it needed a bit of attention before it could be auctioned. He spotted some glue that one of the Sardine Sisters had been using to put on her false eyelashes. Soon he was busily sticking the bits of string in place on the frame.

"Are there any more contestants?" Prawn heard a voice say. He looked up. Judge Salmon was standing at the front of the stage and it looked as though it might be too late. Prawn pushed his way to the front. "Wait!" he cried. "I'd like to try!" The judge looked down. "And what have you got to offer?" he said, casting a cold eye over Prawn's treasure. "I'm going to auction this... thing," mumbled Prawn, struggling on to the stage. "Well, get on with it then," snapped the judge.

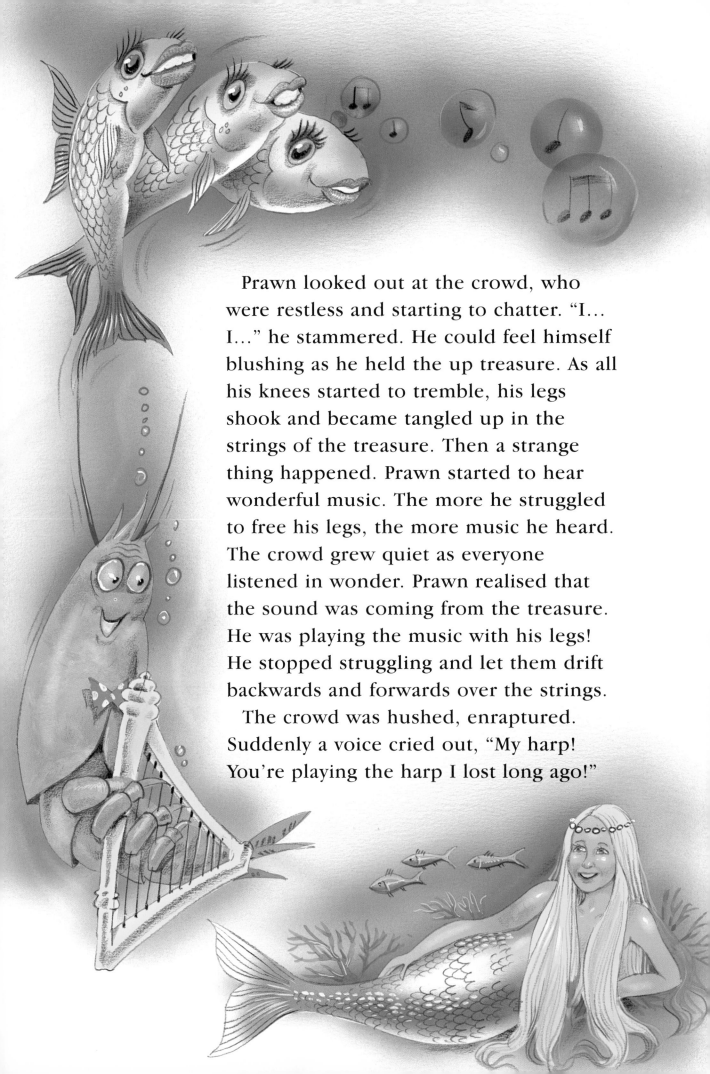

Prawn looked out at the crowd, who were restless and starting to chatter. "I… I…" he stammered. He could feel himself blushing as he held the up treasure. As all his knees started to tremble, his legs shook and became tangled up in the strings of the treasure. Then a strange thing happened. Prawn started to hear wonderful music. The more he struggled to free his legs, the more music he heard. The crowd grew quiet as everyone listened in wonder. Prawn realised that the sound was coming from the treasure. He was playing the music with his legs! He stopped struggling and let them drift backwards and forwards over the strings.

The crowd was hushed, enraptured. Suddenly a voice cried out, "My harp! You're playing the harp I lost long ago!"

Prawn looked up. Mermaid was swimming towards him with tears in her eyes. She rushed up on to the stage and kissed and hugged him for joy. "Thank you, Prawn!" she cried. "You have played the most beautiful music on my harp that I have ever heard." The crowd cheered. Prawn blushed.

"I suppose you could call it a hidden talent," he said.

The Planet Where Time Goes Backwards

Far beyond our solar system,
In the outer reaches of space,
There's a planet where time goes backwards,
And it's the most peculiar place.

A place where birds climb into their shells,
And leaves flutter up to the trees,
Clouds suck rain from out of the ground,
And rivers flow out of the seas.

The cooks wash up at the start of the meal
And unpeel the spuds, I'm told.
Your dinner goes into the oven,
And comes out nice and cold.

On building sites, they start with a house
And take it apart brick by brick,
At lunchtime they spit out their sandwiches
(It looks like they're being sick!)

At petrol pumps they take fuel out of cars,
And football's not much of a laugh:
The match ends with both teams at zero,
And they start by having a bath.

You know something bad's going to happen,
Because someone will start to cry.
But the people get younger each day,
And they greet you by saying "goodbye".

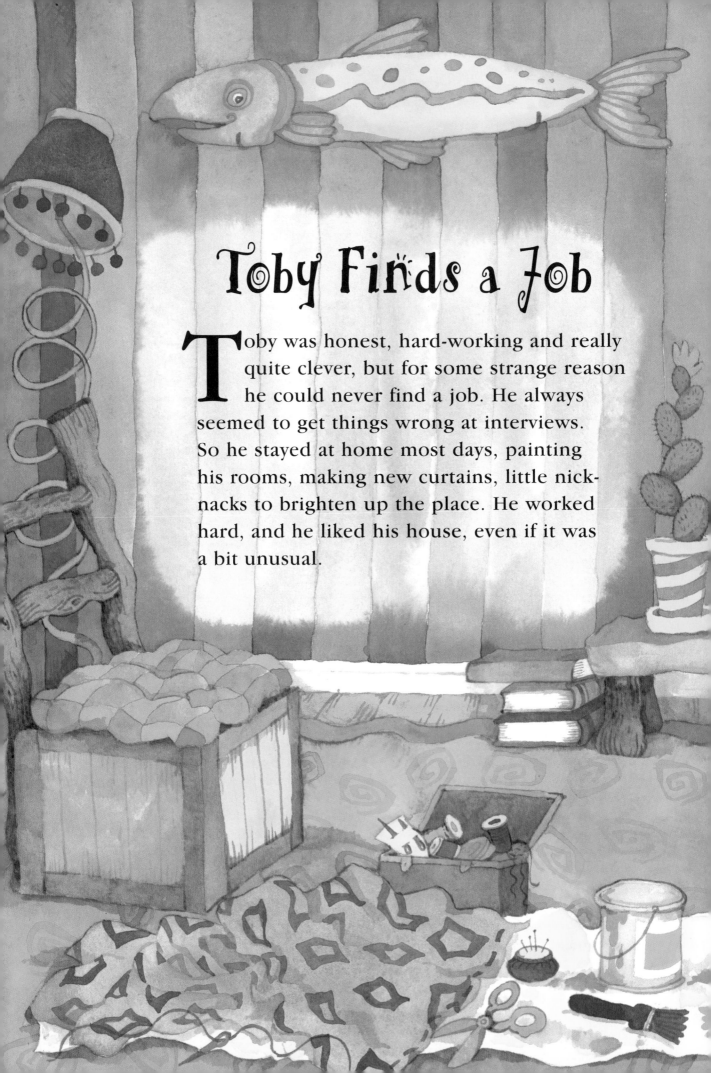

Toby Finds a Job

Toby was honest, hard-working and really quite clever, but for some strange reason he could never find a job. He always seemed to get things wrong at interviews. So he stayed at home most days, painting his rooms, making new curtains, little nick-nacks to brighten up the place. He worked hard, and he liked his house, even if it was a bit unusual.

Toby's friends all knew that Toby was looking for a job and they were always on the lookout for things he could do. One day, his friend Suzie called to say that the office where she worked was looking for a 'spokesperson'.

'A 'spokesperson',' thought Toby. 'It's an odd sort of job, but I think I can do it.' He went to his shed and took the wheels off his bicycle. Then he went to all his friends and borrowed their bicycle wheels too. By lunchtime he had lots of wheels and hundreds of spokes. He went along to the company and said:

"I'm very good with spokes! See? I've got long ones, short ones, bent ones, but most of them are straight."

The interviewer scratched his head and laughed. "No, a 'spokesperson' is someone who talks to people – newspapers, radio and television. They tell them what the company does. It's got nothing to do with bicycle wheels."

"Oh," said Toby, and he went home again and made a new coffee table out of a big drainpipe.

The following day, Toby's friend Sam called to say that the school down the road was looking for someone to help out. "The person they need," he said, "must be good with children." But Toby didn't hear him right. He thought that Sam had said 'chickens'.

'Chickens?' thought Toby. 'In a school? That's most unusual, but perhaps they're learning about farms or perhaps they have a pets corner.'

So he went to a nearby chicken farm and borrowed as many chickens as he could fit into his car. Then he went to the school.

"I've come about the job," said Toby, unloading the chickens. The chickens ran all over the classroom, squawking and clucking. Feathers flew everywhere and the children screamed and huddled into a corner.

"Get those chickens out of here," said the teacher angrily.

It took Toby a long time to round up the chickens and by that time the teacher looked so cross that Toby thought it better not to ask for a job. He went home and painted his kitchen yellow with green spots.

A couple of days later, Toby's friend Jeremy telephoned to say that his company was looking for a fundraiser, did he want to do that?

'A fun dresser,' thought Toby afterwards. 'Now that's the job for me. I've always enjoyed dressing up in bright and unusual clothes, but I wonder what a fun dresser does at work. Perhaps he just goes around cheering everyone up.'

Toby went to his wardrobe. He had built it himself out of driftwood from the beach and old dustbin lids.

Toby chose his funniest clothes: a Viking helmet with horns sticking out of it, a shirt covered with frills and fancy trimmings, a pair of baggy trousers covered with bright patches, his flippers, a tie like a fish and, to complete the outfit, his wizard's cape, covered with stars and signs of the zodiac. He wasn't sure if others would think this was a fun thing to wear or not; it was the kind of thing he wore all the time.

When Toby got to the interview he leapt into the room with a loud, "Ta-daaa," and was greeted by stunned silence. The people in the office were very smartly dressed in white shirts and grey suits and just sat there with their mouths open.

"Is this not fun enough?" asked Toby, surprised by their silence.

"I beg your pardon," said a stiff-looking lady with a notepad.

"Is this the kind of fun dressing you had in mind?" asked Toby. "I've got more like this at home."

The ladies and gentlemen in their suits looked at each other with puzzled expressions and then one of them laughed. Then they all laughed.

"No," one of them said at last, gulping for air. "We're looking for a 'fundraiser,' you know, someone who raises money."

"Oh," said Toby, feeling very foolish indeed. "Not someone who dresses in funny clothes?"

"Not really," said the man, laughing so much his sides hurt.

Toby went home on the bus, trying not to worry about the funny looks he was getting from the other passengers.

A few days later, all of Toby's friends came to visit him. Sam was there, and Suzie and Jeremy.

They were worried about Toby. Would he ever find a job? Toby was excited to have all his friends round.

"You sit there, Suzie," he said. "It's my new inflatable chair. I made it myself out of car inner-tubes."

"Wow! It's great!" laughed Suzie. "It really is very comfortable."

"This chair is good, too," said Jeremy, sitting on one Toby had made out of old packing cases.

The friends chatted and laughed. They loved Toby, but they thought his job-hunting mistakes were really quite funny.

"What about that time you went for a job as a book-keeper," laughed Suzie, "with all those books under your arm."

"Well, I've got lots of books," said Toby, bashfully. "I'm very good at keeping them."

"Yes, but a book-keeper looks after money, not books," said Suzie.

"I know that now," said Toby.

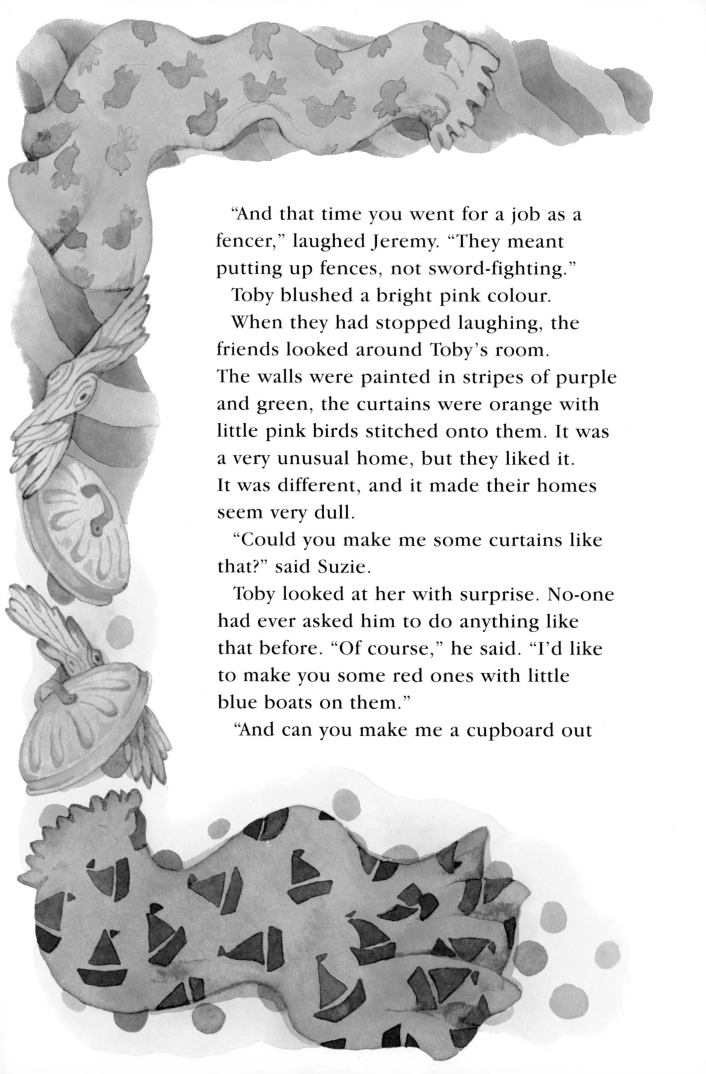

"And that time you went for a job as a
fencer," laughed Jeremy. "They meant
putting up fences, not sword-fighting."

Toby blushed a bright pink colour.

When they had stopped laughing, the
friends looked around Toby's room.
The walls were painted in stripes of purple
and green, the curtains were orange with
little pink birds stitched onto them. It was
a very unusual home, but they liked it.
It was different, and it made their homes
seem very dull.

"Could you make me some curtains like
that?" said Suzie.

Toby looked at her with surprise. No-one
had ever asked him to do anything like
that before. "Of course," he said. "I'd like
to make you some red ones with little
blue boats on them."

"And can you make me a cupboard out

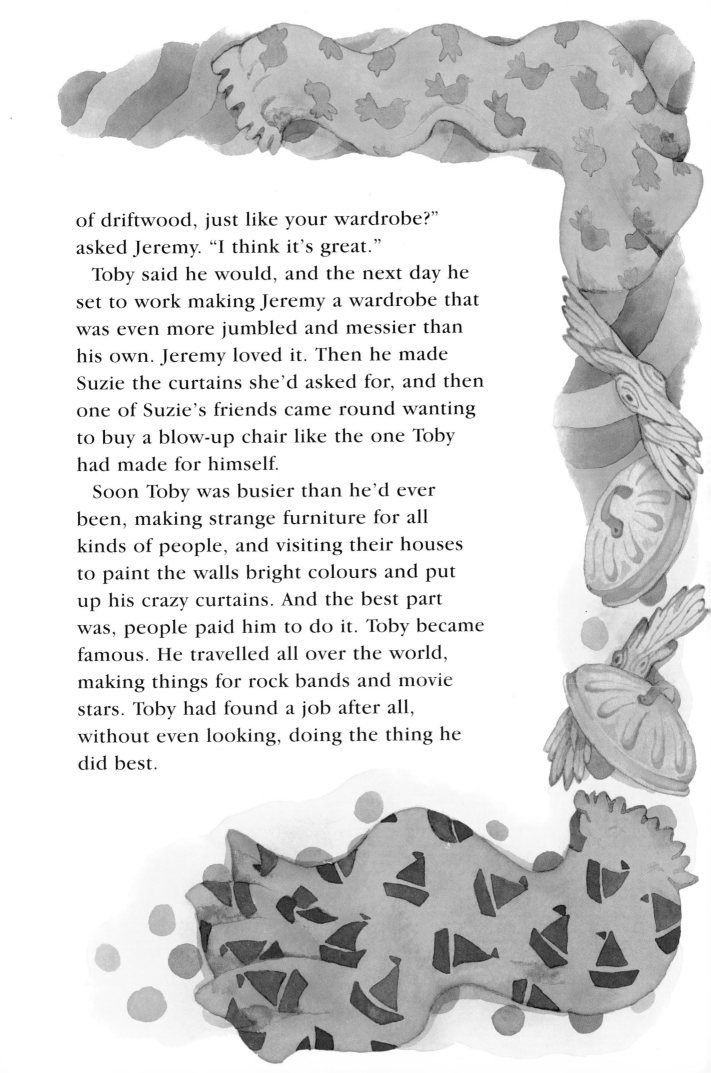

of driftwood, just like your wardrobe?" asked Jeremy. "I think it's great."

Toby said he would, and the next day he set to work making Jeremy a wardrobe that was even more jumbled and messier than his own. Jeremy loved it. Then he made Suzie the curtains she'd asked for, and then one of Suzie's friends came round wanting to buy a blow-up chair like the one Toby had made for himself.

Soon Toby was busier than he'd ever been, making strange furniture for all kinds of people, and visiting their houses to paint the walls bright colours and put up his crazy curtains. And the best part was, people paid him to do it. Toby became famous. He travelled all over the world, making things for rock bands and movie stars. Toby had found a job after all, without even looking, doing the thing he did best.

A Knight to Remember

Long, long ago, when kings ruled over kingdoms, fearsome dragons terrorised the lands and beautiful princesses swooned over dashing knights in shining armour, there lived a very worried man called Alfred Ramsbottom.

Alfred was a great big bear of a man, with an important job working as chief blacksmith to the king. He shod the king's horses, and equipped his knights with swords, shields and suits of armour.

Business had been very good recently because the kingdom where Alfred lived was being menaced by a large and loathsome dragon, who had seen off every valiant knight that had set out to slay him. Alfred could barely keep up with the workload, as knight after knight prepared to be sent into battle. Things were so bad that the king had to put up a banner on the castle walls, which read:

Knights wanted. Must be brave, dashing and fearless. Experience in dragon-slaying an advantage. Competitive salary, plus the hand of the princess upon defeat of the dragon.

All eligible young men should apply to the castle at the earliest opportunity.

But there had only been three applicants. They had all made very tasty breakfasts for the dragon, who was looking forward to more.

So, you are probably wondering, just what was worrying Alfred? Was it the heavy workload?

Was it the dragon? Was he worried that the king would send him out to slay the dragon? Well, you won't be able to guess, so I'll tell you... it was his son, Nigel.

Now, Nigel was as different from his dad as it was possible to be. He was small, he was weedy, he had soft, smooth hands. Worse still, he liked music, and poetry and... knitting! He'd happily sit by the fire with his mother for hours on end, needles clicking away as he worked on a nice new tunic. There was no chance of him joining the family business– he couldn't even lift his father's hammers! Just the night before Nigel had overheard his parents talking:

"What will become of the boy?" groaned Alfred. "All he does is sit around the house all day singing and playing his lute. And as for the knitting– what good is that going to do him? How will he ever be able to make his way in the world?"

"Now, now, dear," soothed his wife. "Don't worry. We musn't lose hope. He may surprise us yet!"

Poor Nigel, being the sensitive chap that he was, was mortified to discover that he was a disappointment to his parents, and he decided to give them the surprise of their lives!

Nigel had seen the king's advertisement, and while he'd been knitting, he'd been thinking. He wasn't big and butch, but he was quick and clever. He'd come up with a plan to outsmart that mean old dragon, and now was the time to put it into action...

The king could hardly keep a straight face when Nigel presented himself at court, bowed low before the throne and declared himself at the king's service. What hope did a measly little shrimp like this have of defeating the dragon? Still, beggars can't be choosers, thought the king, and in the absence of other offers, he took up his sword and knighted Nigel without delay.

"Good luck," smiled the princess, peeping out shyly from behind her father's throne. She rather liked the look of this one. He was a change from the great hairy brutes she'd seen so far.

Alfred was shocked when Nigel presented himself and his horse to be kitted out for battle. Now he really had something to worry about! But for all his worries about his son, he loved him dearly, and begged him to reconsider.

"How can you hope to win?" Alfred pleaded. "You'll be a bite-sized snack for this dragon!"

"Don't worry, Dad," soothed Nigel. "You want me to make my way in the world – and that's just what I intend to do! Besides, I have a cunning plan!" With a mysterious smile, he opened his knapsack to reveal his lute, two large knitting needles and a huge ball of wool! Poor Alfred looked at his son in puzzlement and dismay, but before he had time to ask questions, Nigel leaped onto his horse and rode away into the forest.

For four long days and nights nothing
more was heard of him.

While his parents sat anxiously at home,
Nigel was very busy indeed. When he arrived
at the dragon's lair, he hid himself in a small
crack in the rock at the mouth of the dragon's
cave. He waited till he heard the dragon snoring
away deep in the depths, then took out his
knitting needles and the huge ball of wool.
His needles flashed as he worked furiously, and
in no time at all he had knitted a huge net that
stretched across the entire mouth of the cave.
Then he took out his lute and, perching high
on a rock above the cave, he began to play the
sweetest song he knew.

Now, not many people know this, but dragons
can't stand music or poetry. It jangles their
nerves, and their skin crawls and their teeth
grind. But Nigel knew, so it was no surprise
to him that his plan worked like a dream.

On hearing the gentle melody, the dragon came roaring towards the mouth of the cave, nostrils flaring and flames shooting, which is just what Nigel had hoped he'd do.

The flames singed a hole in the middle of the net, which was just big enough for the dragon's head to slip through as he charged towards it. Before he knew where he was, the net had slipped over him like a jumper, and he was well and truly tangled up and held fast. He writhed and struggled, but Nigel's knitting held firm! Then came the next part of the plan.

With the dragon held captive, Nigel took up his lute once more, and serenaded him with the soppiest, silliest love songs he knew. And when he got bored, he recited poetry – long odes to lost loves that drove the dragon to distraction. For four days and

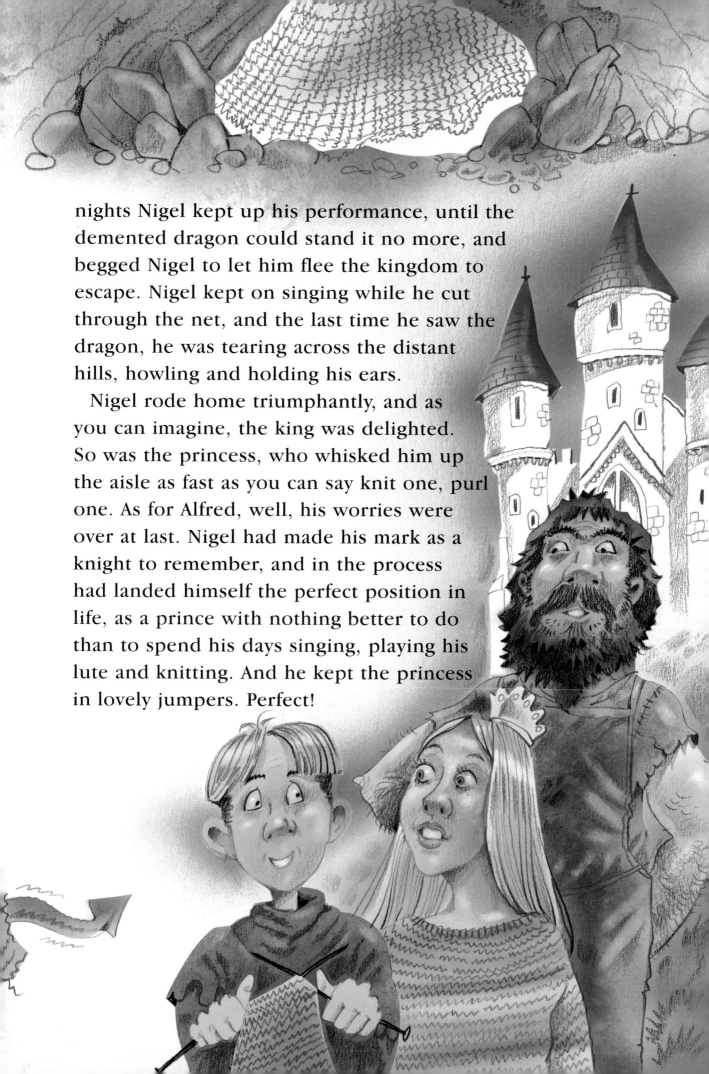

nights Nigel kept up his performance, until the demented dragon could stand it no more, and begged Nigel to let him flee the kingdom to escape. Nigel kept on singing while he cut through the net, and the last time he saw the dragon, he was tearing across the distant hills, howling and holding his ears.

Nigel rode home triumphantly, and as you can imagine, the king was delighted. So was the princess, who whisked him up the aisle as fast as you can say knit one, purl one. As for Alfred, well, his worries were over at last. Nigel had made his mark as a knight to remember, and in the process had landed himself the perfect position in life, as a prince with nothing better to do than to spend his days singing, playing his lute and knitting. And he kept the princess in lovely jumpers. Perfect!

A Whale of a Time

Did you hear the story
Of Wendy Bligh,
The remarkable whale
Who loved to fly?

It happened like this:
She was sleeping one day
When a hot-air balloonist
Flew her way.

He looked down below
And spotted her hump,
"I'll land on that rock,"
Said he, with a thump.

He tied up his balloon
With a beautiful bow,
While Wendy slept on –
She just didn't know.

Then a big tornado
Whirled over the sea.
It blew Wendy upwards
As high as could be.

"What a wonderful feeling!"
The whale cried in glee.
"I am floating above
The sparkling blue sea."

The hot-air balloonist
Took her for a spin.
She chatted to sea birds
And waved her great fin.

He dropped her back home
At the end of the day.
"Oh thank you!" she smiled
And then swam away.

Good Homes Wanted

"Meow, meow!" A large black-and-white cat sat on the garden wall outside number three Cherry Tree Avenue, watching and waiting. At four o'clock precisely a schoolboy appeared at the corner of the road and the cat arched its back and purred excitedly as its friend approached.

"Hello puss," said the boy, whose name was Danny. "Been waiting long?"

"Meow, meow," replied the cat, which meant, 'since half past ten this morning.'

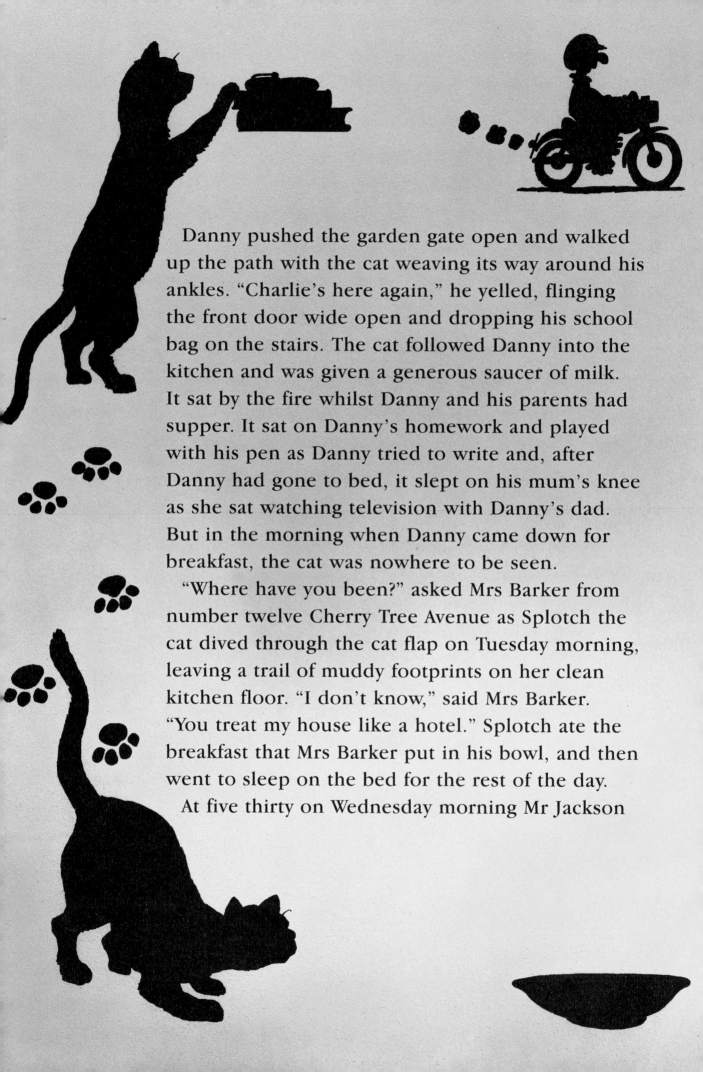

Danny pushed the garden gate open and walked up the path with the cat weaving its way around his ankles. "Charlie's here again," he yelled, flinging the front door wide open and dropping his school bag on the stairs. The cat followed Danny into the kitchen and was given a generous saucer of milk. It sat by the fire whilst Danny and his parents had supper. It sat on Danny's homework and played with his pen as Danny tried to write and, after Danny had gone to bed, it slept on his mum's knee as she sat watching television with Danny's dad. But in the morning when Danny came down for breakfast, the cat was nowhere to be seen.

"Where have you been?" asked Mrs Barker from number twelve Cherry Tree Avenue as Splotch the cat dived through the cat flap on Tuesday morning, leaving a trail of muddy footprints on her clean kitchen floor. "I don't know," said Mrs Barker. "You treat my house like a hotel." Splotch ate the breakfast that Mrs Barker put in his bowl, and then went to sleep on the bed for the rest of the day.

At five thirty on Wednesday morning Mr Jackson

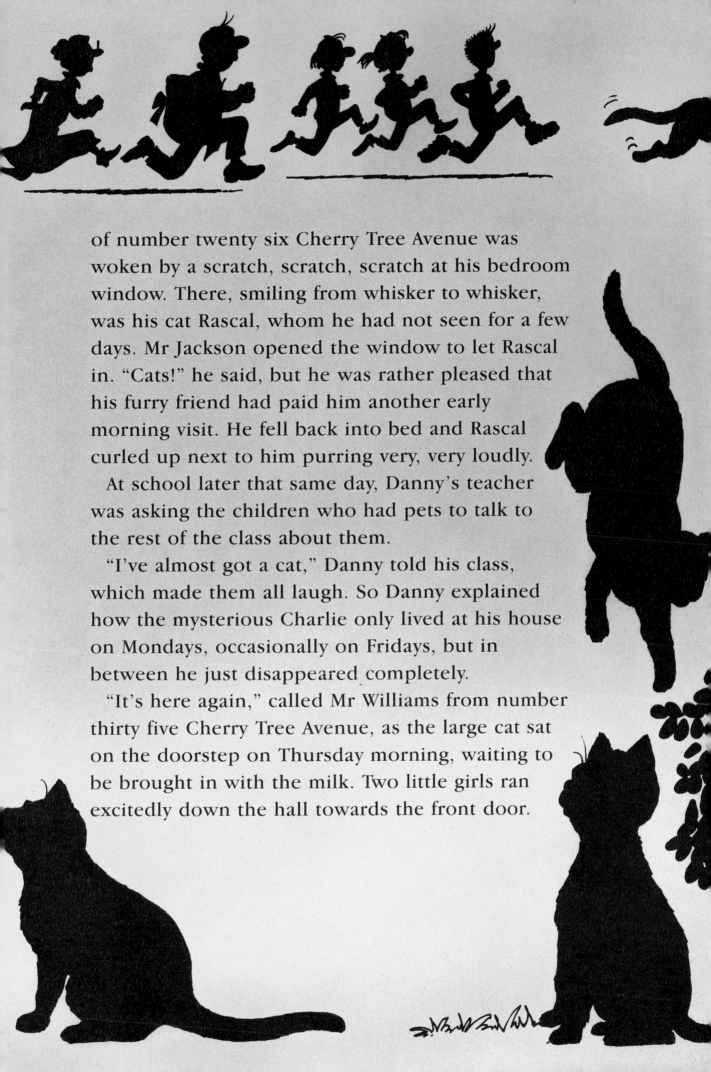

of number twenty six Cherry Tree Avenue was woken by a scratch, scratch, scratch at his bedroom window. There, smiling from whisker to whisker, was his cat Rascal, whom he had not seen for a few days. Mr Jackson opened the window to let Rascal in. "Cats!" he said, but he was rather pleased that his furry friend had paid him another early morning visit. He fell back into bed and Rascal curled up next to him purring very, very loudly.

At school later that same day, Danny's teacher was asking the children who had pets to talk to the rest of the class about them.

"I've almost got a cat," Danny told his class, which made them all laugh. So Danny explained how the mysterious Charlie only lived at his house on Mondays, occasionally on Fridays, but in between he just disappeared completely.

"It's here again," called Mr Williams from number thirty five Cherry Tree Avenue, as the large cat sat on the doorstep on Thursday morning, waiting to be brought in with the milk. Two little girls ran excitedly down the hall towards the front door.

"Oh please let him in, Daddy," cried Suzy, the older of the two girls.

"I want to hold him," said Jenny, pushing her sister aside. Mr Williams tucked his morning paper under one arm. "Now girls, no squabbling, or you'll frighten it," he said. But there was little chance of that. Mr Williams opened the door just a little and the cat rushed in rolling around on the rug enjoying the little girls' attention.

"Can we keep him?" asked Suzy.

"He could sleep on my bed," suggested Jenny helpfully.

"No, mine," insisted Suzy, and another argument broke out.

"Girls, girls," said Mrs Williams, appearing at the top of the stairs in her dressing gown. "Oh, look," she beamed as she spotted the cat. "He's come back. Do you think he'd like some bacon?" The cat rolled onto its back and pedalled an imaginary bicycle which meant,

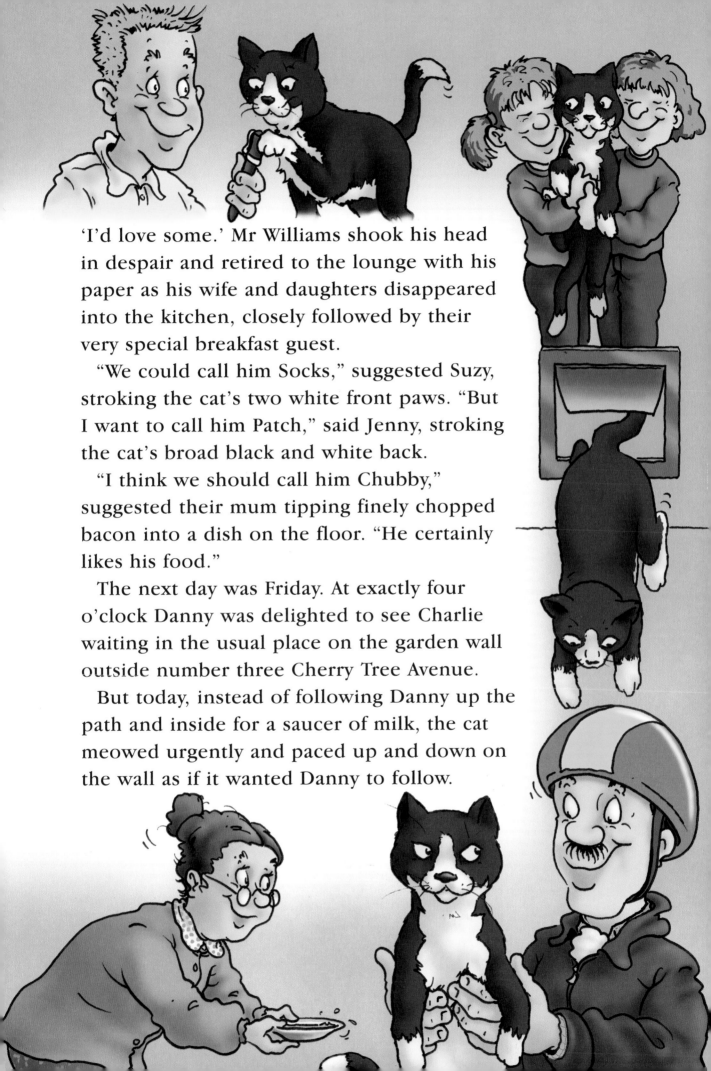

'I'd love some.' Mr Williams shook his head in despair and retired to the lounge with his paper as his wife and daughters disappeared into the kitchen, closely followed by their very special breakfast guest.

"We could call him Socks," suggested Suzy, stroking the cat's two white front paws. "But I want to call him Patch," said Jenny, stroking the cat's broad black and white back.

"I think we should call him Chubby," suggested their mum tipping finely chopped bacon into a dish on the floor. "He certainly likes his food."

The next day was Friday. At exactly four o'clock Danny was delighted to see Charlie waiting in the usual place on the garden wall outside number three Cherry Tree Avenue.

But today, instead of following Danny up the path and inside for a saucer of milk, the cat meowed urgently and paced up and down on the wall as if it wanted Danny to follow.

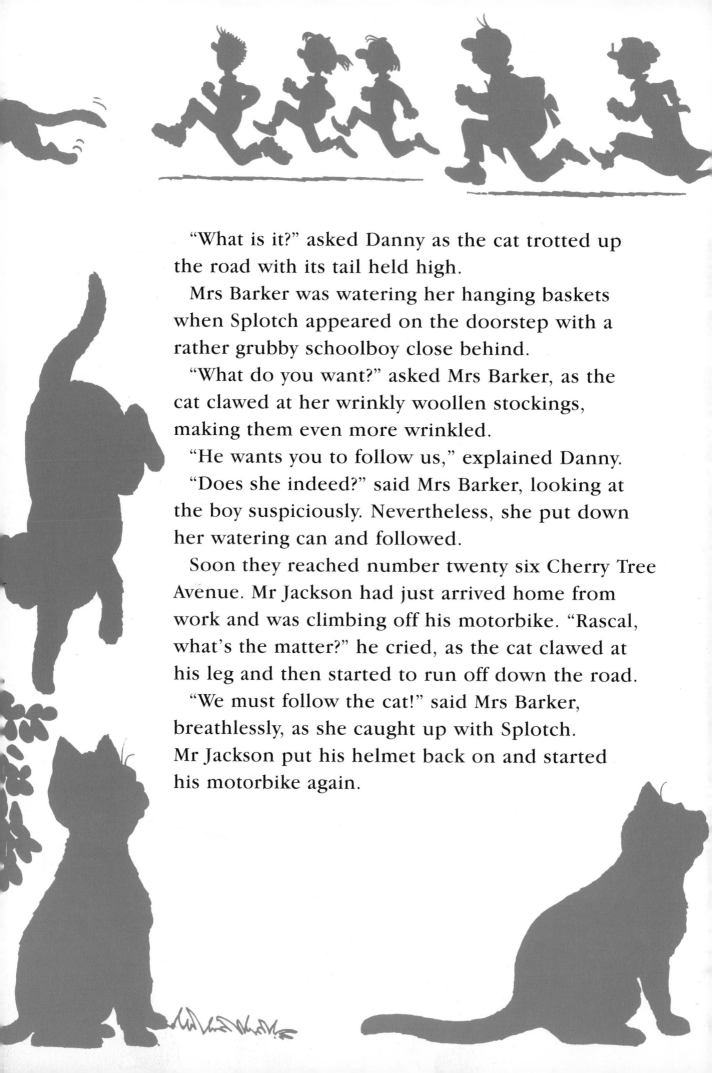

"What is it?" asked Danny as the cat trotted up the road with its tail held high.

Mrs Barker was watering her hanging baskets when Splotch appeared on the doorstep with a rather grubby schoolboy close behind.

"What do you want?" asked Mrs Barker, as the cat clawed at her wrinkly woollen stockings, making them even more wrinkled.

"He wants you to follow us," explained Danny.

"Does she indeed?" said Mrs Barker, looking at the boy suspiciously. Nevertheless, she put down her watering can and followed.

Soon they reached number twenty six Cherry Tree Avenue. Mr Jackson had just arrived home from work and was climbing off his motorbike. "Rascal, what's the matter?" he cried, as the cat clawed at his leg and then started to run off down the road.

"We must follow the cat!" said Mrs Barker, breathlessly, as she caught up with Splotch. Mr Jackson put his helmet back on and started his motorbike again.

He wobbled off after Rascal with Danny and Mrs Barker trying desperately to keep up.

"Nyawww," went the bike as it turned the corner into Market Street. "Meow, meow," said the cat as it spotted Mr Roe the Fishmonger.

"Well I never," said Mr Roe in surprise when he saw the strange line of people trying to keep up with a cat. Curiosity got the better of him, and he thought he had better join in– he might be missing out on something!

The cat then ran through the market closely followed by Mr Jackson and Mr Roe with Danny and poor old Mrs Barker bringing up the rear.

Stallholders gazed in amazement as the cat and its pursuers disappeared around the corner into the adventure playground.

Mrs Williams was pushing her two daughters on the swings.

"Look, it's Socks!" cried Suzy.

"No, it's Patch," corrected Jenny, and they both jumped off the swings and followed Mr Jackson, Mr Roe, Danny and Mrs Barker whose woollen stockings were now very very wrinkly indeed!

At last, and much to everyone's relief, the cat stopped. They all looked at each other, feeling rather awkward and embarrassed, and then they all looked down at the cat. She seemed to be smiling as with her nose she gently made a gap in the hedge to reveal six beautiful black and white kittens. Kittens all ready and waiting for their new owners to take them to their purrrrrrfect new homes.

Oscar the Octopus

Oscar the Octopus put on a boot,
Stretched out a tentacle, ready to shoot.
Oscar the Octopus put on a second,
It took far longer than Oscar had reckoned.
Oscar the Octopus put on boot three,
A crowd had just gathered to watch by the sea,
Waving and singing in anticipation,
Of Oscar, the latest goal-scoring sensation.
Oscar the Octopus put on boot four,
He felt on top form and was longing to score.
Oscar the Octopus put on boot five,
The match was a big one and televised live.
The crowd were all swaying and shouting and cheering,

And hoping that Oscar would soon be appearing.
Oscar the Octopus put on boot six,
And stood on his head as he practised some kicks.
Oscar the Octopus put on boot seven,
And straightened his shirt – he was number eleven.
He gazed in the mirror and felt really proud,
It was time for his debut in front of the crowd.
Just one more boot – would he ever be ready?
The laces were fiddly, his nerves were unsteady.
Oscar the Octopus put on boot eight,
Walked on to the pitch but the Ref said, "Too late.
The game is all over, the whistle has blown,
Nobody scored and the crowd has gone home."

Steve and Stella

"Give that present to me!" Steve shouted at his sister Stella. "It's much better than my one!" He launched himself angrily at her and made a grab for the model dinosaur she had just been given by Father Christmas, who was sitting at the end of Santa's Grotto in a big department store. Stella stepped swiftly aside and Steve crashed straight into a model of Rudolph the Red Nosed Reindeer, complete with flashing nose. It swayed, then fell, bringing the Christmas tree down, too. Decorations went flying, and waiting children ran away, shrieking, for safety.

Steve and his sister Stella quarrelled all the time and it drove their parents mad.

Steve and Stella always felt hard done by. If one was given a present, the other would fly into a rage, either because he or she didn't have one or because they thought it was better than theirs. Often it ended in a fight and usually, the present got broken.

Their fight in Santa's Grotto was one of their worst battles. They had a severe telling off from their parents and had to clear up the mess they had made, paying for the damage out of their pocket money. But it made no difference. They still carried on quarrelling.

Then, one day, something so extraordinary happened to them that they never, ever quarrelled again.

It was a Saturday, and it started out like any other Saturday – with an argument.

Steve and Stella had decided go fishing. They had started to argue, however, about who would use the best fishing rod first. They were both standing by the stream at the bottom of their

garden, calling for their mother and shouting
"I want it!" "No, no, I want it!" at the tops of
their voices.

"Be quiet, both of you," snapped their mother.
"If you can't stop arguing, you will have to fish
with it together. Just don't break it!" And with
that warning, she went back to the house.

So Steve and Stella both grabbed the same rod
and cast the line out into the stream.

They both felt the tug at the end of it at the
same time.

"Wow!" breathed Steve. "That's a sharp pull.
I reckon we've hooked something really big."

For once, Stella agreed with him.

They reeled it in. There was a flash of brilliant
green, as a long, wriggling eel-like shape flew out
of the stream and splashed down onto the grass
at their feet.

"What on earth is it?" gasped Stella, bending
over for a closer look. Then she shrieked in
amazement. "It looks human!"

"Don't be daft," sighed Steve. But as he pushed
Stella aside he had a shock.

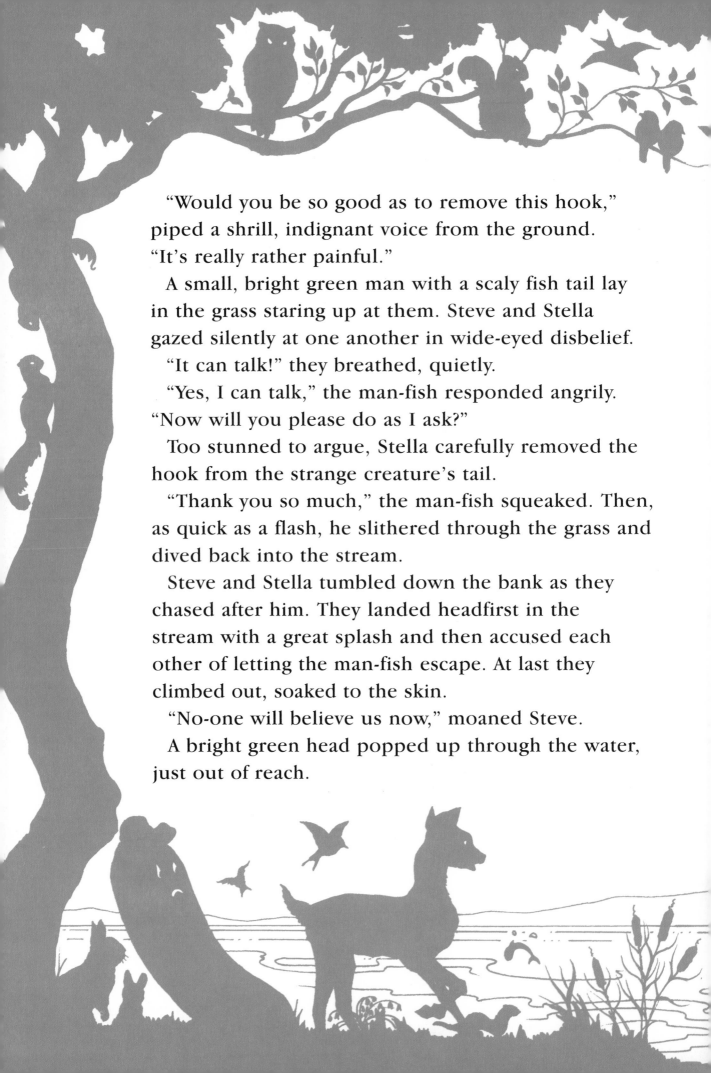

"Would you be so good as to remove this hook," piped a shrill, indignant voice from the ground. "It's really rather painful."

A small, bright green man with a scaly fish tail lay in the grass staring up at them. Steve and Stella gazed silently at one another in wide-eyed disbelief.

"It can talk!" they breathed, quietly.

"Yes, I can talk," the man-fish responded angrily. "Now will you please do as I ask?"

Too stunned to argue, Stella carefully removed the hook from the strange creature's tail.

"Thank you so much," the man-fish squeaked. Then, as quick as a flash, he slithered through the grass and dived back into the stream.

Steve and Stella tumbled down the bank as they chased after him. They landed headfirst in the stream with a great splash and then accused each other of letting the man-fish escape. At last they climbed out, soaked to the skin.

"No-one will believe us now," moaned Steve.

A bright green head popped up through the water, just out of reach.

"I almost forgot," the man-fish called to them. "I grant you three wishes for catching me and then letting me go."

He disappeared beneath the water and was never seen again.

Steve and Stella looked at one another. Were they dreaming? Had they really been granted three wishes?

"I've read about this kind of thing in fairy stories," said Steve doubtfully. "But everyone knows that's all make-believe."

"Well, it can't be make-believe, can it?" Stella retorted. "What about the little green man? He was a fairy tale creature alright."

Steve agreed that they had actually hooked a creature that could talk and was half man and half fish. "But I bet you're wrong about the wishes," he scoffed.

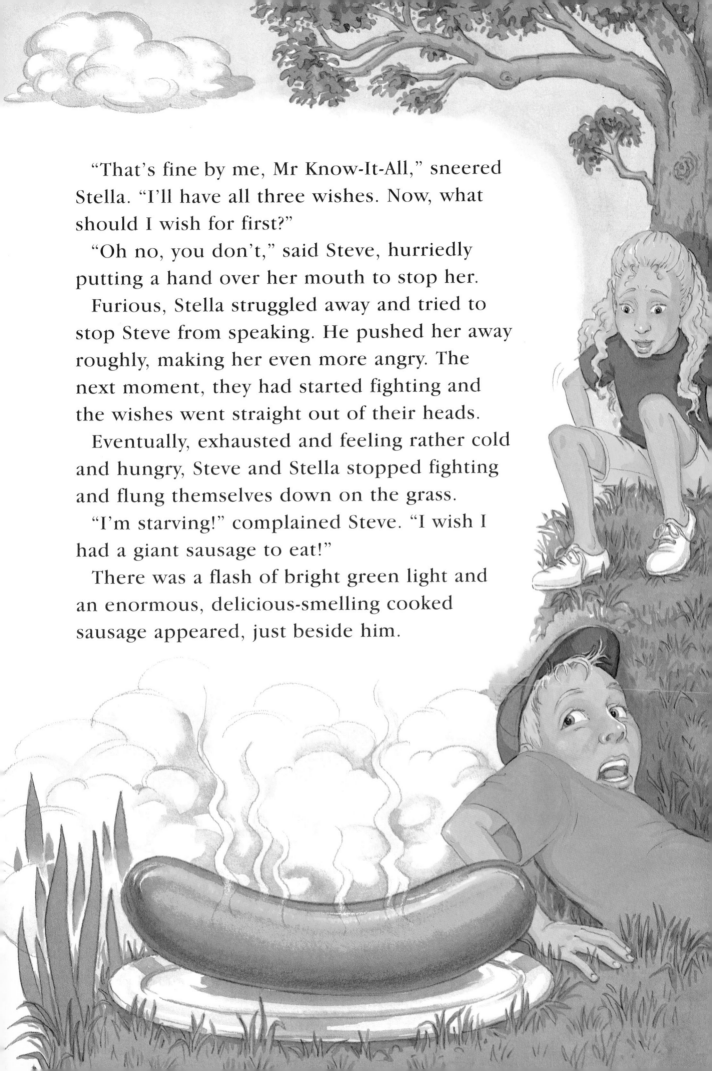

"That's fine by me, Mr Know-It-All," sneered Stella. "I'll have all three wishes. Now, what should I wish for first?"

"Oh no, you don't," said Steve, hurriedly putting a hand over her mouth to stop her.

Furious, Stella struggled away and tried to stop Steve from speaking. He pushed her away roughly, making her even more angry. The next moment, they had started fighting and the wishes went straight out of their heads.

Eventually, exhausted and feeling rather cold and hungry, Steve and Stella stopped fighting and flung themselves down on the grass.

"I'm starving!" complained Steve. "I wish I had a giant sausage to eat!"

There was a flash of bright green light and an enormous, delicious-smelling cooked sausage appeared, just beside him.

Steve and Stella stared at it, unable to believe their eyes and too amazed to speak.

Stella was the first to recover.

"You silly idiot! You've wasted a precious wish!" she screamed at her brother, beside herself with rage. "I wish you were that stupid sausage! That would teach you a lesson!"

Stella froze in horror, realising– too late– what she had just done. With a bright green flash, her brother turned into a giant sausage.

It was an astonishing sight, a sausage the size of a tree trunk lying on the grass beside her. The sausage was dressed in the tatters of Steve's clothes. His baseball cap was now perched on one end of the sausage, which made it look even more ridiculous.

Then it started moaning.

"Help me! I don't want to be a sausage!" came the faint sound of Steve's voice from deep down inside the sausage.

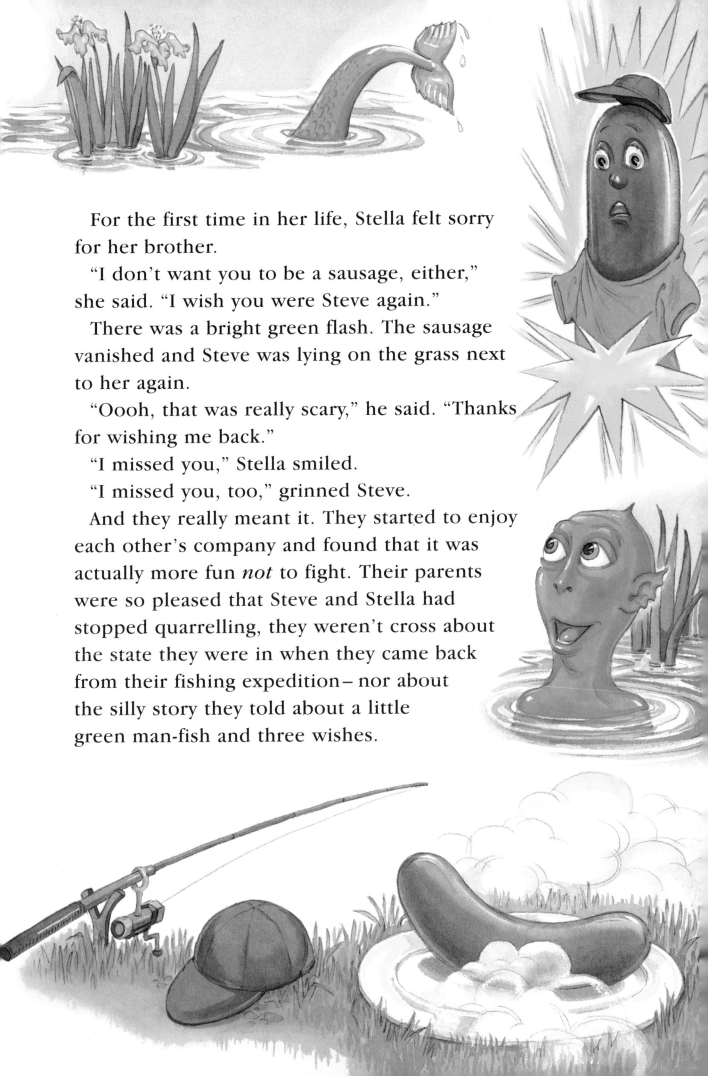

For the first time in her life, Stella felt sorry for her brother.

"I don't want you to be a sausage, either," she said. "I wish you were Steve again."

There was a bright green flash. The sausage vanished and Steve was lying on the grass next to her again.

"Oooh, that was really scary," he said. "Thanks for wishing me back."

"I missed you," Stella smiled.

"I missed you, too," grinned Steve.

And they really meant it. They started to enjoy each other's company and found that it was actually more fun *not* to fight. Their parents were so pleased that Steve and Stella had stopped quarrelling, they weren't cross about the state they were in when they came back from their fishing expedition – nor about the silly story they told about a little green man-fish and three wishes.

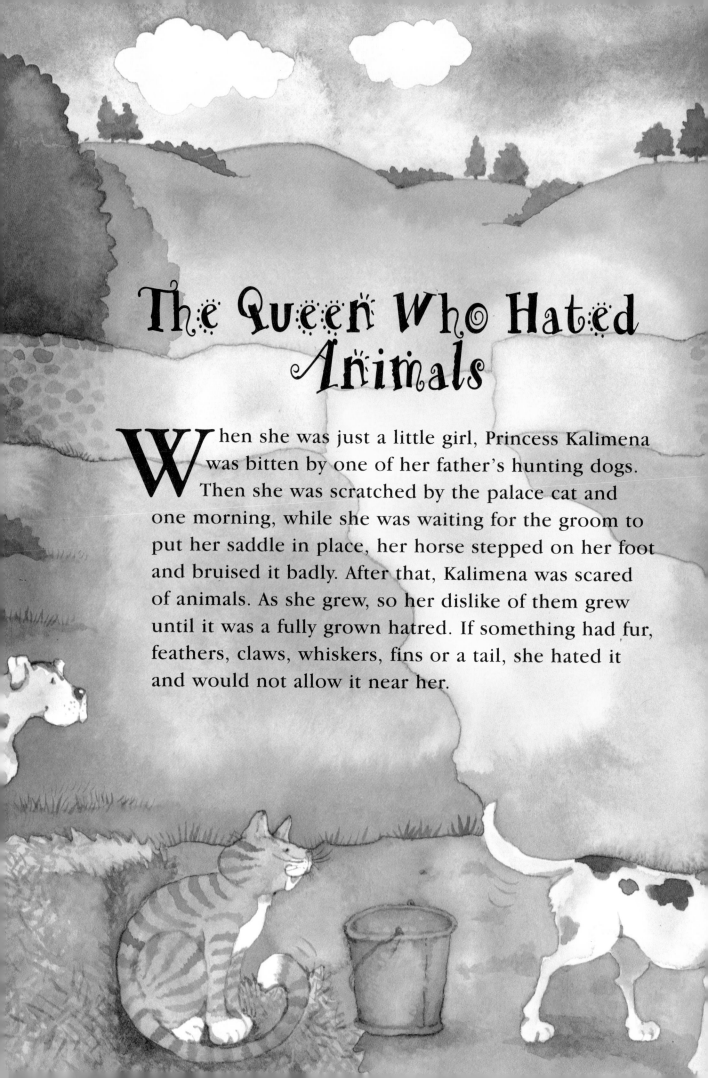

The Queen Who Hated Animals

When she was just a little girl, Princess Kalimena was bitten by one of her father's hunting dogs. Then she was scratched by the palace cat and one morning, while she was waiting for the groom to put her saddle in place, her horse stepped on her foot and bruised it badly. After that, Kalimena was scared of animals. As she grew, so her dislike of them grew until it was a fully grown hatred. If something had fur, feathers, claws, whiskers, fins or a tail, she hated it and would not allow it near her.

So when Princess Kalimena became Queen Kalimena, the first thing she did was pass a very unpopular new law.

"From this day forth, all animals are banned from the land," she declared.

Now this was not such a difficult thing to do in the palace grounds. The horses were removed from their stables, the dogs were taken out of their cosy kennels and the peacocks were banished from the gardens. But the servants in the palace had a terrible time. Spiders were brushed from the corners, shutters were closed against stray bees, but no matter what they did, woodlice always found a way in.

Out in the kingdom, it was even harder to banish the animals. The people needed their sheep and pigs, and their cows and chickens, and they loved their pets. What's more, how could they possibly banish the birds and snakes, butterflies and rabbits? It was a silly law made by a silly queen, they thought.

However, silly as she was, the Queen was very powerful and had to be obeyed. So the people found a way round the problem. They kept the animals, but disguised them as other things so that the queen and her officials would never know they were still there.

One day, Queen Kalimena decided to take a tour of her land. She rumbled along the country lanes in her carriage, pulled very slowly by four very hot and tired guards.

"Can't you go any faster?" she yelled.

The queen waved to her subjects as they worked in the fields and she was pleased to see that there were no animals. However, some of the people did look very strange. Their clothes didn't fit them at all well and they didn't seem to be doing very much work. And once, when she was passing a hairy-looking scarecrow, she was convinced she heard it bleat like a goat.

When she became hungry, the queen stopped at the nearest house to have lunch. On this particular day, it was the house that belonged to Tasha and her family.

"The queen is coming," warned her father as he rushed into the house. "Are the animals hidden?"

"Yes," replied Tasha. "Just throw the tablecloth over the pig and we'll be ready."

"Now, stand very still," she said to the rabbits on the shelves who were pretending to be bookends. "And you two," she said to the cranes in the corner, "you're supposed to be lamps, remember, so no squawking."

The queen strode in haughtily.

"Your Majesty," said Tasha's mother, curtsying. "How lovely to see you."

"Oh, what a gorgeous shawl," said the queen, looking at two white swans that Tasha's father had hung on a peg with strict instructions not to flap their wings. The queen picked up the swans and draped them over her shoulders. "Oh, it fits me beautifully," she said. "So warm and surprisingly heavy."

She sat down.

Now, the chair that the queen sat in was really a kangaroo with a cloth thrown over him and when she sat down he did his best not to gasp or fidget. Tasha's mother put a wonderful display of food on the table, which was actually the pig, and the queen started to eat and drink.

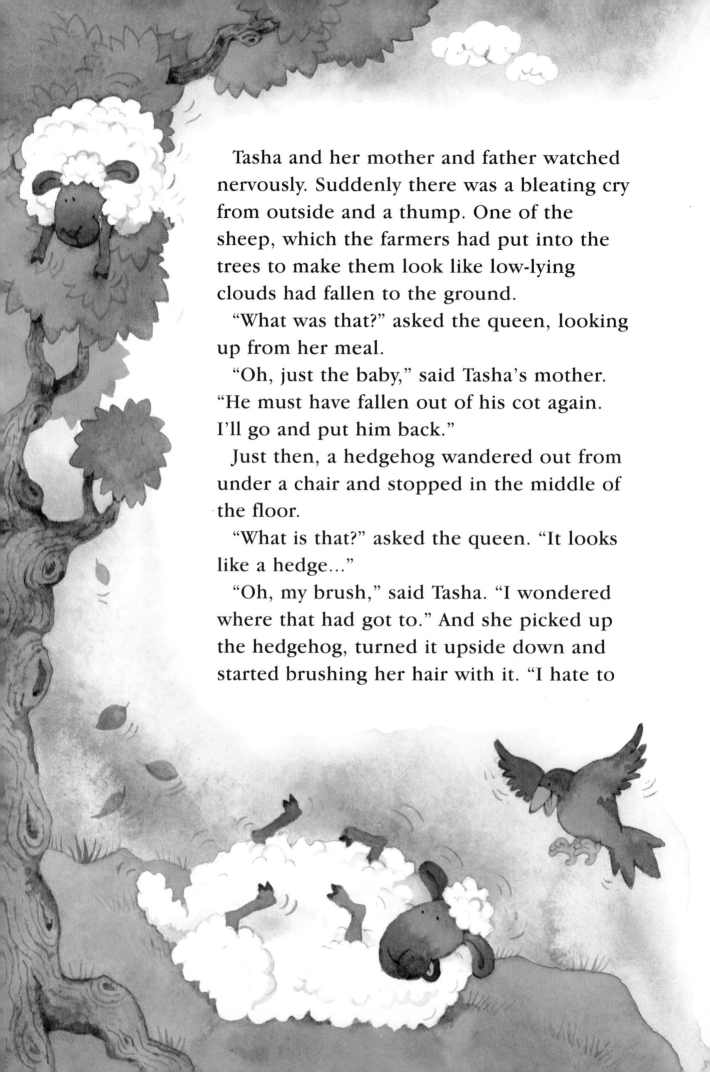

Tasha and her mother and father watched
nervously. Suddenly there was a bleating cry
from outside and a thump. One of the
sheep, which the farmers had put into the
trees to make them look like low-lying
clouds had fallen to the ground.

"What was that?" asked the queen, looking
up from her meal.

"Oh, just the baby," said Tasha's mother.
"He must have fallen out of his cot again.
I'll go and put him back."

Just then, a hedgehog wandered out from
under a chair and stopped in the middle of
the floor.

"What is that?" asked the queen. "It looks
like a hedge..."

"Oh, my brush," said Tasha. "I wondered
where that had got to." And she picked up
the hedgehog, turned it upside down and
started brushing her hair with it. "I hate to

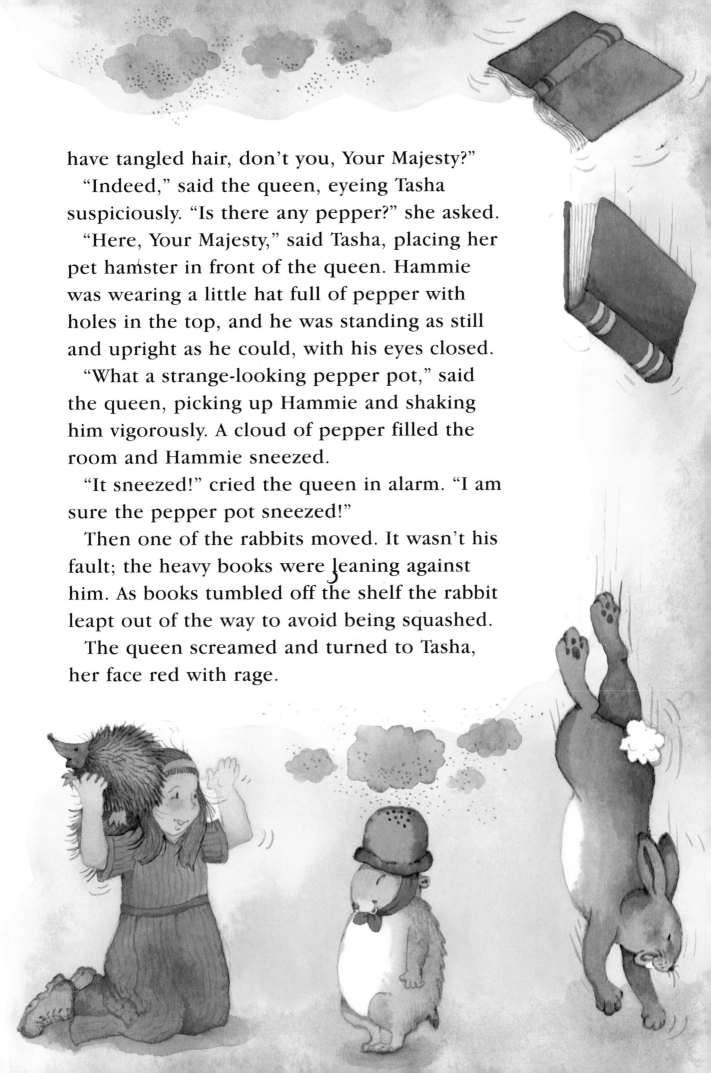

have tangled hair, don't you, Your Majesty?"

"Indeed," said the queen, eyeing Tasha suspiciously. "Is there any pepper?" she asked.

"Here, Your Majesty," said Tasha, placing her pet hamster in front of the queen. Hammie was wearing a little hat full of pepper with holes in the top, and he was standing as still and upright as he could, with his eyes closed.

"What a strange-looking pepper pot," said the queen, picking up Hammie and shaking him vigorously. A cloud of pepper filled the room and Hammie sneezed.

"It sneezed!" cried the queen in alarm. "I am sure the pepper pot sneezed!"

Then one of the rabbits moved. It wasn't his fault; the heavy books were leaning against him. As books tumbled off the shelf the rabbit leapt out of the way to avoid being squashed.

The queen screamed and turned to Tasha, her face red with rage.

"You know I have banned animals!" she yelled, and stamped her foot hard, right on the kangaroo's foot. That was enough for the poor kangaroo. He started bounding around the room, with the queen clinging on for dear life. Squealing loudly, the pig ran off and the plates fell crashing to the floor. The cranes squawked and took off out of the window, the lampshades still on their heads. The cat cushions leapt from the chairs, the snake draught-excluders slithered out of the door and the kangaroo bounded out of the house and made for the open country, with Queen Kalimena still clinging on.

"Put me down!" screamed the queen, and finally the kangaroo did – but just then the swans decided it was time to get away.

They flapped their wings and took to the

air, taking the queen with them as they flew. Higher and higher they soared.

"OHHH!" screamed the queen. Then "Oohh," in a slightly different voice. She was flying, which was something she'd always wanted to do. The swans took her high over her kingdom, beating their great white wings and the queen laughed as she swooped low over the palace and the town. When the swans finally brought the queen gently down beside the lake, she was ecstatic with joy.

Her court officials ran outside.

"Shoot the swans," one of them shouted.

"No," cried the queen. "Let them live. Let all the animals live. They are wonderful."

So the swans returned to the lake, the rabbits went back to their burrows, the sheep climbed gratefully down from the trees, and they all lived properly ever after.

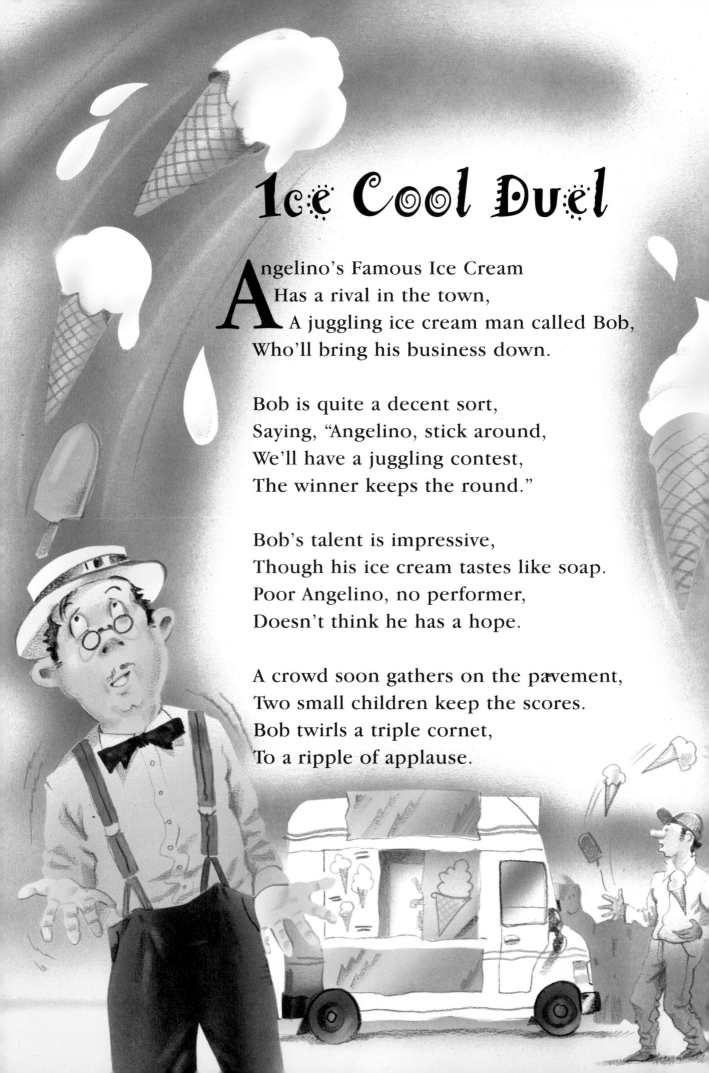

Ice Cool Duel

Angelino's Famous Ice Cream
Has a rival in the town,
A juggling ice cream man called Bob,
Who'll bring his business down.

Bob is quite a decent sort,
Saying, "Angelino, stick around,
We'll have a juggling contest,
The winner keeps the round."

Bob's talent is impressive,
Though his ice cream tastes like soap.
Poor Angelino, no performer,
Doesn't think he has a hope.

A crowd soon gathers on the pavement,
Two small children keep the scores.
Bob twirls a triple cornet,
To a ripple of applause.

Angelino keeps his cool, though,
Knows that he will be just fine.
What goes up a plain old cornet,
Comes down a lemon'n'lime.

Bob hates the thought of losing,
Reaches down towards his knees,
Pulls out a cherry-flavoured ice-pop,
Tells Angelino, "Time to *freeze*!"

But Angelino has his measure,
So he plays his final trick.
Bob falls, knocked out cold,
By a large vanilla brick!

Smoky and the Salsa Class

Smoky the dragon was feeling depressed. What was wrong with the world? There had been a time when a young dragon was usefully employed fighting knights and giants, or imprisoning princesses.

Those were the days, reflected Smoky as he remembered how he had defeated that buck-toothed oaf Sir Justin Tyme and his knock-kneed squire Soupwithsaltin, and how he had struck terror into the heart of Princess Esmerelda when he had tried to rescue her.

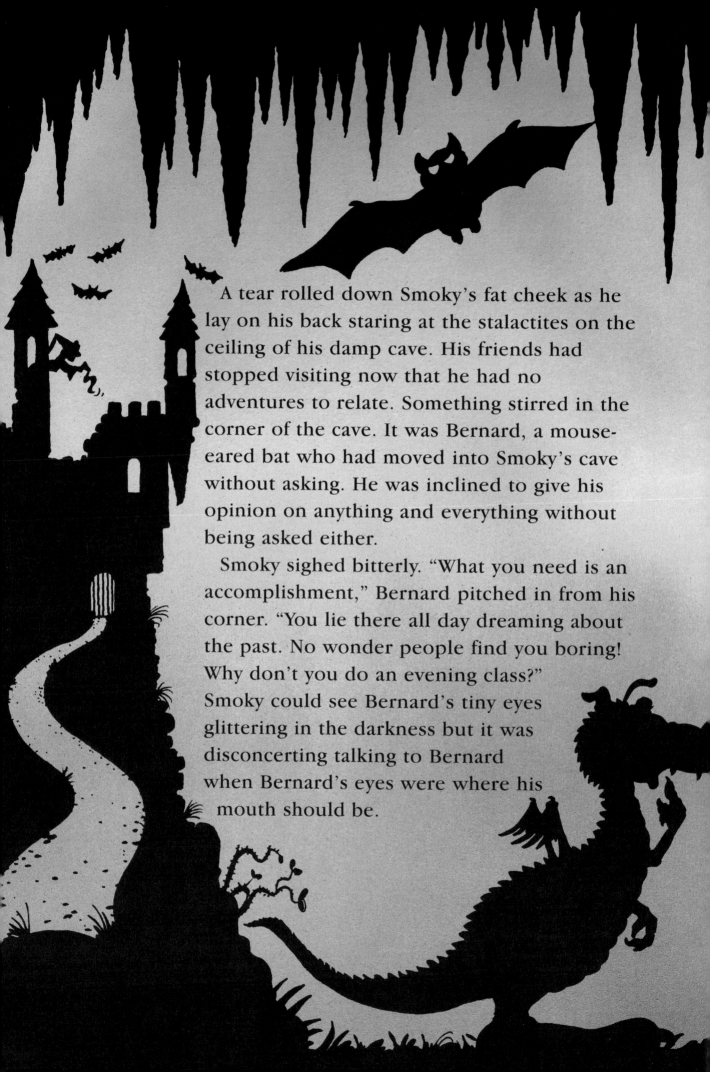

A tear rolled down Smoky's fat cheek as he lay on his back staring at the stalactites on the ceiling of his damp cave. His friends had stopped visiting now that he had no adventures to relate. Something stirred in the corner of the cave. It was Bernard, a mouse-eared bat who had moved into Smoky's cave without asking. He was inclined to give his opinion on anything and everything without being asked either.

Smoky sighed bitterly. "What you need is an accomplishment," Bernard pitched in from his corner. "You lie there all day dreaming about the past. No wonder people find you boring! Why don't you do an evening class?" Smoky could see Bernard's tiny eyes glittering in the darkness but it was disconcerting talking to Bernard when Bernard's eyes were where his mouth should be.

"Oh, I wouldn't be any good at classes!" snapped Smoky crossly. But he had to admit that Bernard had a point. It would be a good way to keep busy and make new friends.

The very next day, Smoky left his cave for the first time in ages and flew down to the local town. He was rather out of practice at flying and landed inside the library, rather than outside as he had intended, which caused a bit of a stir. "Quiet, please!" whispered the librarian fiercely as Smoky crash landed on the carpet in a cloud of dust and debris. "I'd like some information about evening classes," said Smoky. The librarian mopped her brow. Smoky suddenly remembered that he was standing far too close and the poor woman was overheating. He stepped back and the librarian handed him a leaflet. "If it catches fire, you'll have to pay for a replacement," she grumbled.

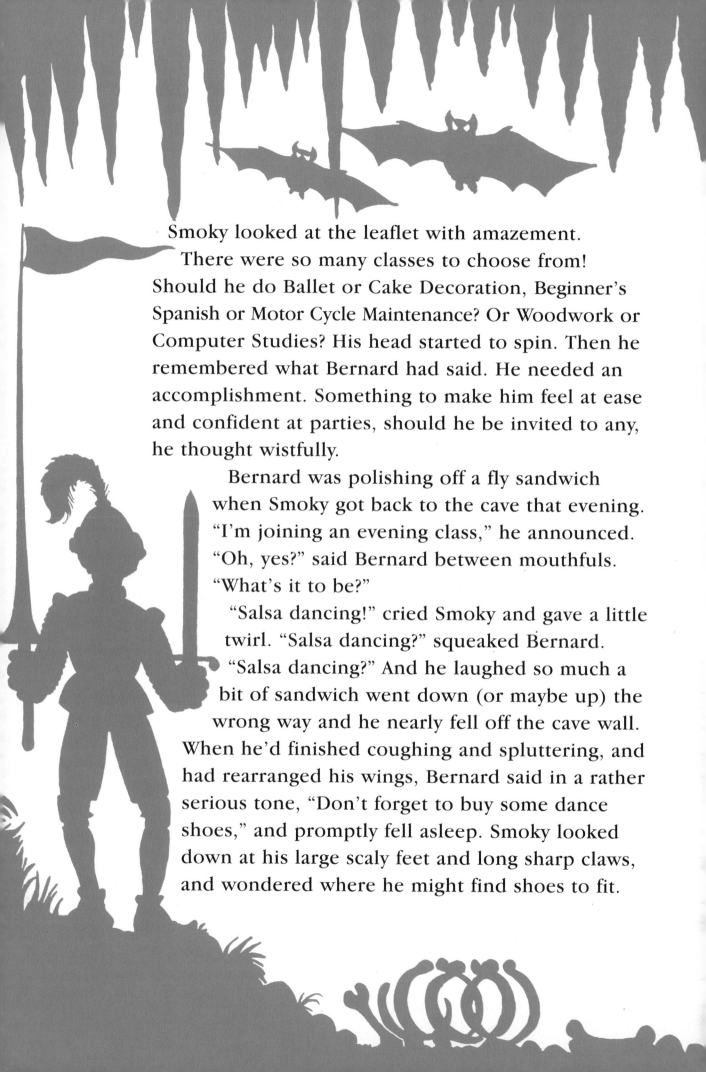

Smoky looked at the leaflet with amazement.

There were so many classes to choose from! Should he do Ballet or Cake Decoration, Beginner's Spanish or Motor Cycle Maintenance? Or Woodwork or Computer Studies? His head started to spin. Then he remembered what Bernard had said. He needed an accomplishment. Something to make him feel at ease and confident at parties, should he be invited to any, he thought wistfully.

Bernard was polishing off a fly sandwich when Smoky got back to the cave that evening. "I'm joining an evening class," he announced. "Oh, yes?" said Bernard between mouthfuls. "What's it to be?"

"Salsa dancing!" cried Smoky and gave a little twirl. "Salsa dancing?" squeaked Bernard.

"Salsa dancing?" And he laughed so much a bit of sandwich went down (or maybe up) the wrong way and he nearly fell off the cave wall. When he'd finished coughing and spluttering, and had rearranged his wings, Bernard said in a rather serious tone, "Don't forget to buy some dance shoes," and promptly fell asleep. Smoky looked down at his large scaly feet and long sharp claws, and wondered where he might find shoes to fit.

The next day, Smoky flew down to the
High Street in the hope of finding a shoe
shop that specialised in footwear for dragons.
After a fruitless search, he decided he
would have to try an ordinary shoe shop
and ventured into *Booted and Spurred*.

"I'd like a pair of dance shoes," Smoky said
to the assistant. The man looked down at
Smoky's huge feet and suppressed a giggle.
"Exactly what sort of dancing did sir have in
mind?" he asked. "Salsa dancing," replied
Smoky. "Oh, that's alright sir! I think you'll
find people wear all sorts of shoes for salsa
dancing," explained the man. "What about
bare feet?" asked Smoky anxiously. "Well,"
said the assistant, "I think you'll be fine as
your feet are quite..." he hesitated,
"erm...tough."

Before he knew it, it was time for
Smoky to make his way to the town hall
for his first class. He felt rather nervous as
he approached the hall. What would people
think of him? Would they mind dancing
with a bare-footed dragon? Perhaps they'd
all be scared and run away. He stepped into
the room and looked about him. Then his
jaw dropped in amazement. The room was
full of extraordinary folk all chattering away.
There was a witch in conversation with a
king, an ogre roaring with laughter and
slapping an elf on the back and a knight in
full armour chatting up a princess.

"Welcome, welcome!" said a voice. "You're
new aren't you?" Smoky turned round to see
the teacher approaching him with an
outstretched hand.

He knew it must be the teacher because he was the only ordinary human in the room. He was dressed in tight black trousers, a white shirt and the shiniest black shoes that Smoky had ever seen. "I'm Mr di Magico. What's your name?" asked the teacher. "Smoky," said Smoky.

"Well, Smoky" said Mr di Magico, "We'll be making a start in a minute, but do mingle first," and he was off to greet a timid-looking prince at the door.

Smoky heard a clattering noise as the knight struggled towards him. "Smoky, old mate!" boomed a pompous voice from under the visor. "Long time, no see!" Smoky was puzzled. He didn't recognise the voice. Then he caught sight of a pair of buck teeth. It was Sir Justin Tyme! Smoky felt rather abashed as he thought of how savagely

they had once fought, and hung his head.
"Don't worry, old bean!" chuckled Sir
Justin. "That was long ago. Now we're
all friends!" He clasped Smoky in a noisy
embrace. Smoky could feel bits of metal
sticking into him but he didn't complain.
He was just glad to have a friend.

"Find a partner, everyone!" Mr di Magico
called out and clapped his hands. Smoky
rather hoped that he might partner one of
the pretty princesses but he was swept
onto the dance floor by a wild witch. He
didn't find the dancing easy, mainly because
he kept treading on the witch's black boots
and leaving scratch marks with his claws.
At first he was worried that she might cast a
spell on him, but he soon realised that the
witch was enjoying herself, spinning
around so that her tattered black skirt flew.

"And change!" called Mr di Magico. Suddenly, there was confusion as everyone changed partners. There was plenty of "Sorry, old chap!" "May I...?" and "No, after you!" before Smoky found that he was now indeed dancing with one of the princesses. Not once did she look at Smoky. She kept her eyes fixed firmly on the floor and counted out the rhythm under her breath. Smoky decided that actually the witch was much more fun to dance with.

All too soon the class was over and Smoky flew back to his cave exhausted but happy. From the dark corner, Bernard opened one eye. "How did it go?" he enquired. "It was wonderful!" exclaimed Smoky. "I danced with three princesses, a queen and a witch.

I think I'm in love with the witch," he added.

"Yes, yes," snapped Bernard impatiently, "But what about the salsa dancing?"

"Oh the dancing," said Smoky sheepishly. "I wasn't very good at it. My big feet, you see. But they're having an end-of-term barbecue," he continued and started to grin. "And I'm certainly going to set that on fire!"

The Dotty Professor

"I've built my machine!" cried Professor Von Bean
"It's finished and ready to go!
The greatest invention I've had cause to mention!
It can trundle and suck and it blows!

"The wheels are half green – the wildest you've seen!
The levers all stick out at the side!
It takes just one flick of the switch on this stick
And you'll hear all the gears go inside!

"It's got stripy red panels and lovely blue flannels
And a huge great big pipe on the roof!
The coal goes in here and the smoke goes out there
And instead of a 'toot', it goes woof!

"The door's made of glass and the floor's made of grass!
There's flowers and plants on the back!
There's a cupboard inside that's really quite wide,
So there's somewhere to hang your wet mac!"

Von Bean was delighted and very excited
And happily burst into song.
But his assistant was flustered and suddenly blustered,
"I think that something is wrong!"

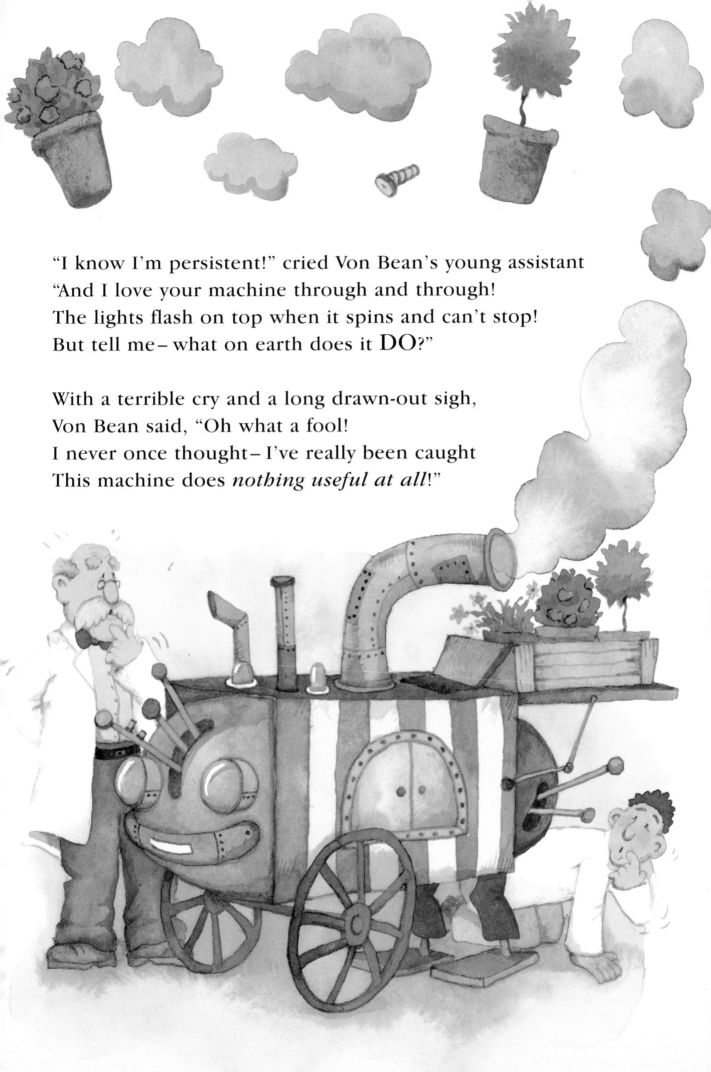

"I know I'm persistent!" cried Von Bean's young assistant
"And I love your machine through and through!
The lights flash on top when it spins and can't stop!
But tell me – what on earth does it DO?"

With a terrible cry and a long drawn-out sigh,
Von Bean said, "Oh what a fool!
I never once thought – I've really been caught
This machine does *nothing useful at all*!"

The Flying Contest

It was a hot day on the African savannah when the animals saw that a notice had been pinned to the trunk of a tree. They gathered around to read it.

The animals stared at the poster in bewilderment. "Ostrich's doing the judging, eh?" guffawed Lion. "What would he know about flying? Why, he can't even fly himself..."

Lion's voice was drowned out by the sound of an aeroplane passing overhead. The animals looked up at the sky and one by one they began to have ideas about how to build their flying machines.

'What a flying machine needs is a noisy engine,' thought Hippo, as he trundled away to the river.

'No flying machine is complete without a tail,' thought Giraffe, as she galloped across the plain.

'The most important things on a flying machine are the wings,' thought Lion wisely, as he stole away through the grass.

But Ellie the elephant just couldn't think of how she would possibly make a flying machine. Ellie was dreadfully forgetful, unlike most elephants – and she had already forgotten what an aeroplane looked like!

'It must have had wings,' she thought, 'so I'd better make myself some. Now let me see...' Ellie tried to remember which creatures she knew that had wings.

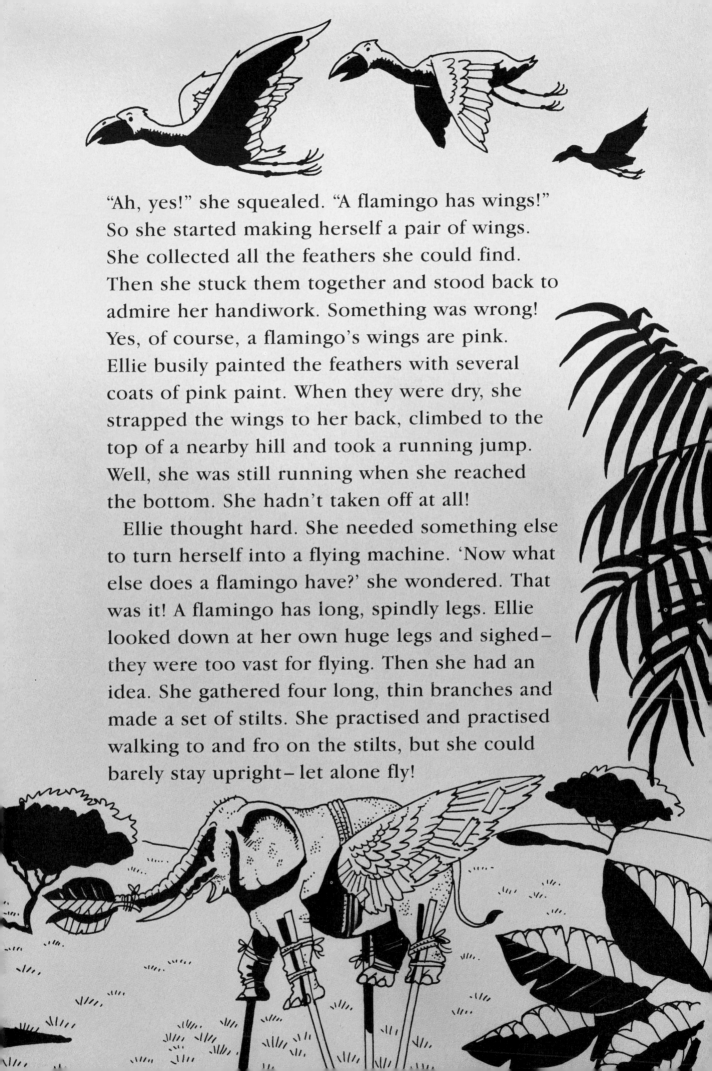

"Ah, yes!" she squealed. "A flamingo has wings!"
So she started making herself a pair of wings.
She collected all the feathers she could find.
Then she stuck them together and stood back to
admire her handiwork. Something was wrong!
Yes, of course, a flamingo's wings are pink.
Ellie busily painted the feathers with several
coats of pink paint. When they were dry, she
strapped the wings to her back, climbed to the
top of a nearby hill and took a running jump.
Well, she was still running when she reached
the bottom. She hadn't taken off at all!

Ellie thought hard. She needed something else
to turn herself into a flying machine. 'Now what
else does a flamingo have?' she wondered. That
was it! A flamingo has long, spindly legs. Ellie
looked down at her own huge legs and sighed –
they were too vast for flying. Then she had an
idea. She gathered four long, thin branches and
made a set of stilts. She practised and practised
walking to and fro on the stilts, but she could
barely stay upright – let alone fly!

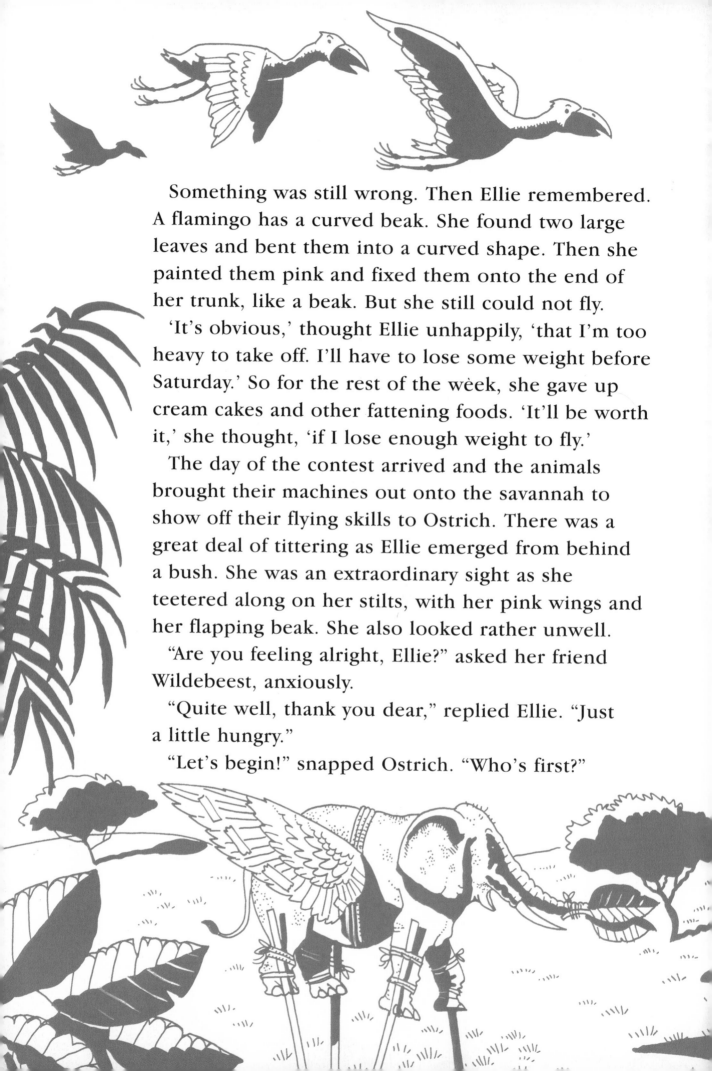

Something was still wrong. Then Ellie remembered. A flamingo has a curved beak. She found two large leaves and bent them into a curved shape. Then she painted them pink and fixed them onto the end of her trunk, like a beak. But she still could not fly.

'It's obvious,' thought Ellie unhappily, 'that I'm too heavy to take off. I'll have to lose some weight before Saturday.' So for the rest of the week, she gave up cream cakes and other fattening foods. 'It'll be worth it,' she thought, 'if I lose enough weight to fly.'

The day of the contest arrived and the animals brought their machines out onto the savannah to show off their flying skills to Ostrich. There was a great deal of tittering as Ellie emerged from behind a bush. She was an extraordinary sight as she teetered along on her stilts, with her pink wings and her flapping beak. She also looked rather unwell.

"Are you feeling alright, Ellie?" asked her friend Wildebeest, anxiously.

"Quite well, thank you dear," replied Ellie. "Just a little hungry."

"Let's begin!" snapped Ostrich. "Who's first?"

"I am!" cried Hippo, leaping into the seat of his machine. "What a flying machine needs is noise!" he shouted over the roar of the engine. It really was a magnificent machine. It looked a bit like a lawn mower with huge, shiny pistons.

"Isn't there something missing?" mused Cheetah with a smile.

But Hippo wasn't listening. "Here we go!" he cried, letting out the throttle as the machine shot off across the savannah in a cloud of black smoke. Faster and faster went the machine but it didn't take off, of course, because it had no wings.

"Ha, ha!" laughed the animals with glee, as it smashed into a tree and Hippo climbed out looking disgruntled.

"Who's next?" asked Ostrich.

"Oh, I am," said Giraffe. "What a flying machine really needs is a tail," she said, as she climbed into her machine. It was spectacular, with a gleaming metal tail standing proudly at the back. She cantered off across the savannah, four legs sticking out of the machine. Faster and faster she galloped, but she didn't take off, because it had no wings.

"Hee, hee!" giggled the animals, as Giraffe's legs got all tangled up and she collapsed in a dizzy heap.

"Who's next?" said Ostrich.

"Meee!" purred Lion smugly. "You foolish animals," he sneered. "What a flying machine needs is wings." And he leaped effortlessly into his machine. The animals gasped in awe. Lion's machine had a simply beautiful pair of silver wings stretching out on either side.

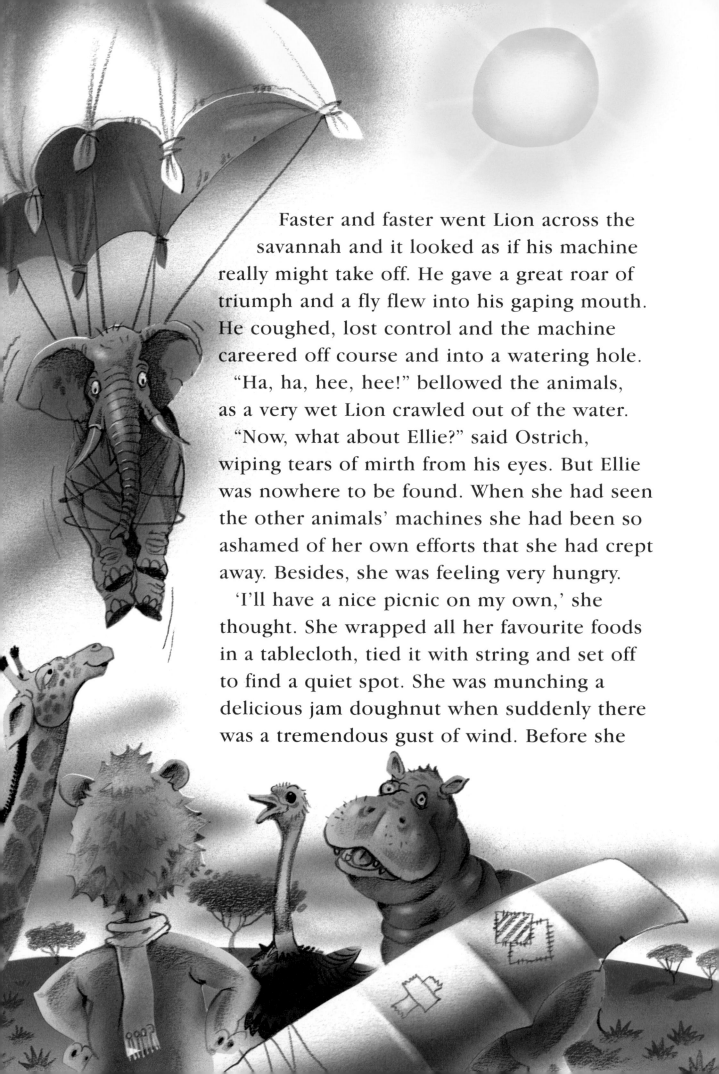

Faster and faster went Lion across the savannah and it looked as if his machine really might take off. He gave a great roar of triumph and a fly flew into his gaping mouth. He coughed, lost control and the machine careered off course and into a watering hole.

"Ha, ha, hee, hee!" bellowed the animals, as a very wet Lion crawled out of the water.

"Now, what about Ellie?" said Ostrich, wiping tears of mirth from his eyes. But Ellie was nowhere to be found. When she had seen the other animals' machines she had been so ashamed of her own efforts that she had crept away. Besides, she was feeling very hungry.

'I'll have a nice picnic on my own,' she thought. She wrapped all her favourite foods in a tablecloth, tied it with string and set off to find a quiet spot. She was munching a delicious jam doughnut when suddenly there was a tremendous gust of wind. Before she could escape, she felt herself being lifted up in the tablecloth and carried high above the trees. She struggled to free herself and got all tangled up in the string.

Just then, the other animals felt the gust too. They looked up into the sky and stared in amazement. They couldn't believe their eyes! Ellie was floating down towards them with the tablecloth and string acting as a parachute!

"Ellie, you're the winner!" announced Ostrich, as she landed on the ground with a soft bump. The other animals cheered and cheered. "It's time to claim your prize – bring out the balloon basket!" called Ostrich. Ellie tried to squeeze her large frame into the basket, but it simply wouldn't fit.

"I'd miss you all anyway," she said. "Why don't we have a picnic together instead? I'm still hungry, as it happens!" So that is exactly what they all did.

The Singing Bank Robber

Bernie McTavish had had a bad day at the office. He hadn't really got anything done all day. Then his wife rang to say that a pipe had burst under the hall floor. Everything was all right, but he would have to climb in through the window, because the furniture was in front of the door.

Bernie put the telephone down with a sigh and put on his black leather motorcycle gear. He couldn't see the bag he usually put his office clothes in, so he found an empty cash bag in the safe and stuffed them into that instead.

Then he set off for home on his motorbike. It was
a dark, damp night. He hadn't gone very far when
the motorbike coughed, juddered and stopped.
Bernie tried to start the engine again, but it was no
good: it was broken. With another deep sigh, Bernie
dismounted, tucked his helmet under his arm and
trudged home. It started to rain.

"Oh, bother," said Bernie.

He was nearly home when he realized that he had a
stone in his boot. It was hurting his foot and making
him limp, but he couldn't be bothered to take it out,
so he limped home, feeling very sorry for himself.
When he got to the house, he eased open the living-
room window, threw the cash bag inside and then
climbed stiffly in after it.

Now, what Bernie didn't realize is that, as
he did this, he was being watched—by two
policemen, in a car across the street.

"Suspicious behaviour!" said one policeman.

"Yes," said the other. "And what's more, he
looks just like that bank robber we're looking for."

Inside the house, Bernie gazed down through the hole in the floor.

"It's OK, Dad," called Jamie. "I've found the leak and I think I can fix it."

"Have a cup of tea, dear," said his wife. "And look what I got for you today. It's part of your fancy dress costume for the party tomorrow night. Try it on."

Bernie tried it on. It was a funny mask, made up of a pair of glasses, a large nose and a fake moustache all joined together.

"Oh, you look terrific," laughed his wife.

Just then there was a loud, insistent knock at the door, and a gruff voice said, "Open up! We know you're in there!"

Bernie and Gladys McTavish looked nervously at each other and started to heave the furniture out of the way.

When they finally managed to open the door, Bernie and Gladys were surprised to see two stern-looking policemen on the doorstep.

"Right, don't move," said the first one. "We have reason to believe, sir, that you are the man who robbed the bank in the high street this afternoon. You don't have to say anything…"

"Me?" cried Bernie. "But I know nothing about any bank robbery."

"You fit the description perfectly, sir. I suggest you take off that foolish disguise. We've got you now."

Bernie took off the mask. "What description?"

"Leathers, slicked-back hair, limp. It's you exactly. Did you think you could evade arrest by barricading yourself into the house, Sir?"

"No," said Bernie. "You see, there's a leak. Jamie's down there now fixing it. We had to move the furniture to get at the floorboards."

"And I suppose," said the second policeman with a grin, "that's why you had to climb into the house through a window."

"Yes, exactly," said Bernie.

The policeman scratched his head and looked doubtful. "And how do you explain the large, and rather full cash bag we saw you with earlier?"

"That was the suit that I wear in the office," said Bernie. "I always change before I come home. And my hair isn't slicked back, it's wet. I got caught in a large downpour."

"This all seems very unlikely, sir," said the first policeman. "How do you explain the bowling ball?"

"Bowling ball?"

"The robber threatened to knock over the bank staff with a bowling ball if they didn't hand over the cash. We clearly saw you with a bowling ball tucked under your arm, sir. You can't escape us."

For a moment Bernie didn't know what on earth they were talking about. Then his face brightened.

"Oh, no," he said. "That's not a bowling ball. That's my motorbike helmet." He showed them the helmet.

"Ah-ha," said the policeman, as if he'd finally found the flaw in Bernie's argument. "But you arrived on foot."

"Yes, my bike broke down," said Bernie. "You see, there's an explanation for everything."

"And the limp?" asked the second policeman, looking more and more puzzled.

"A stone. In my boot," said Bernie. He took off his boot and held it upside-down, and a tiny stone tinkled out onto the floor.

The first policeman whispered something to the second policeman. The second policeman looked doubtful for a moment and then said, "Could you sing for us, sir?"

"Sing?" said Bernie.

"Yes, sing a song for us."

"Anything in particular, Officer?" asked Bernie. He was beginning to think these two policemen were completely mad.

"Something from an opera, sir."

"But I don't know anything from an opera."

"Well, anything will do," said the second policeman.

Bernie took a deep breath and started to sing, "When the red, red, robin comes bob-bob-bobbing along…"

It sounded terrible. Bernie had never been much of a singer. He sounded like a cat stuck in a tree.

"Well, that's it," said the second policeman. "This is the wrong chap. He isn't the bank robber."

"It is?" said the first. "I mean, he isn't?"

"Yes, he isn't."

Everyone looked at the second policeman in complete bewilderment. "Why?" they asked.

"Well, while the staff was filling the cash bag, the robber was singing– something from an opera. And an eye witness…"

"Or an ear witness," suggested Gladys.

"…an ear witness said he sounded quite good. Very good, in fact. So this man, who fits the description in every way, but sings like a parrot with a stomachache, can't possibly be him."

"My singing's not that bad," said Bernie.

"We're sorry to have troubled you, madam," said the first policeman, and as they turned to leave, he added, "I'd get this mess sorted out if I were you."

Bernie sat down heavily on an upturned bucket and sighed. Could things possibly get worse? Just then Jamie appeared through the hole in the floor. He was dripping wet.

"I can't fix the leak, Dad," he said. "There's a lot of water coming in. Have you got a bucket?"

Bernie passed him his motorbike helmet. "Use this," he sighed.

Did You Ever See?

Did you ever see a jester juggling with ice creams,
Or a pair of giant hamsters, wrestling in your dreams?
If you've never seen a crocodile swallow twenty conkers,
Then you, my friend, are totally and utterly quite bonkers!

Did you ever see a puppy dancing with a brolly,
Or a pair of plump old ladies pushing bandits on a trolley?
If you've never seen an elephant sitting on a daisy,
Then you, my friend, are totally and utterly quite crazy!

Did you ever see a piglet all dressed in polka dots,
Or a princess on her wedding day break out in bright green spots?
If you've never been out walking with a pink giraffe named Sad,
Then you, my friend, are totally and utterly quite mad!

Did you ever see a colonel taking tea with a horse,
Or a three-legged mongoose – it's very rare, of course.
If you've never seen a witch's toad looking rather natty,
Then you, my friend, are totally and utterly quite batty!

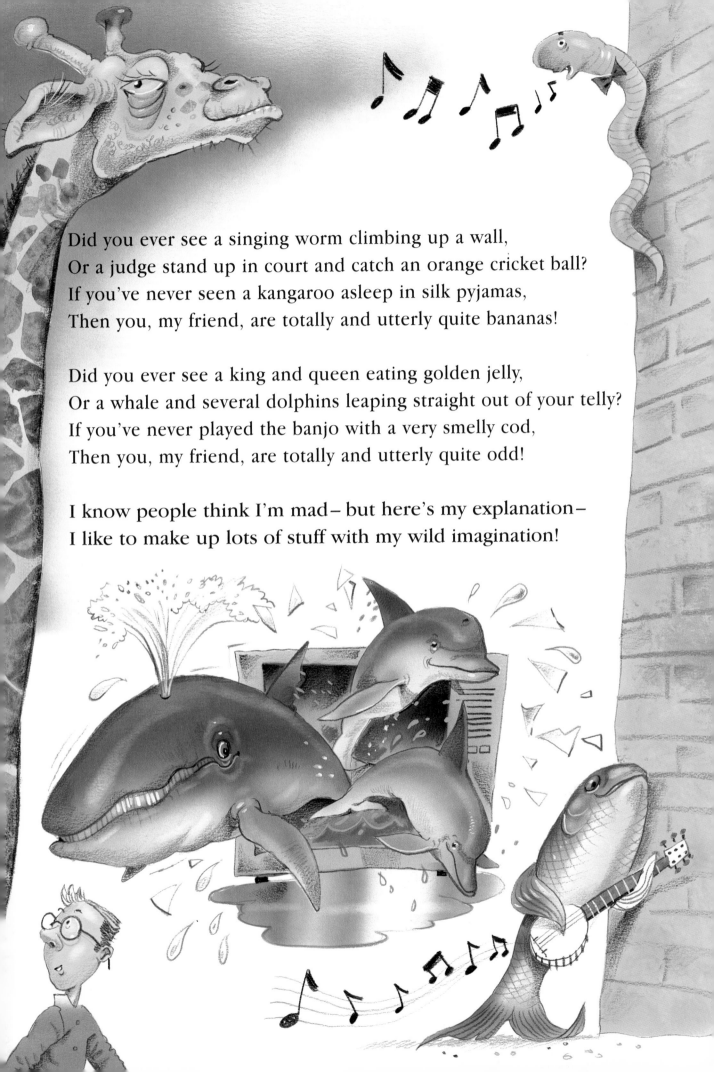

Did you ever see a singing worm climbing up a wall,
Or a judge stand up in court and catch an orange cricket ball?
If you've never seen a kangaroo asleep in silk pyjamas,
Then you, my friend, are totally and utterly quite bananas!

Did you ever see a king and queen eating golden jelly,
Or a whale and several dolphins leaping straight out of your telly?
If you've never played the banjo with a very smelly cod,
Then you, my friend, are totally and utterly quite odd!

I know people think I'm mad – but here's my explanation –
I like to make up lots of stuff with my wild imagination!

The Dog Who Couldn't Bark

Ben gazed into a pair of large brown eyes, and the large brown eyes gazed back. It was a good face, friendly and intelligent, the sort of face that promised fun. Ben liked it immediately. Even though there were seven puppies to choose from, Ben knew that the little brown-and-white one with the funny ears and the curly tail was the one for him.

The puppy began to chase round and round in circles; then he rolled over a couple of times as Ben looked on in amusement and admiration.

"I think I like this one best," announced Ben as the puppy grabbed the sleeve of his jacket and began to tug at it playfully. Ben's dad frowned. As well as being by far the smallest in the litter, the puppy had a floppy ear that fell over his eye whilst the other stuck straight up in the air. And his tail curled round and round, just like a pig's. "He's rather small," Ben's dad pointed out, and the little puppy doubled his height by standing on his back legs and springing around the kitchen as if he were on a pogo stick.

"Please…" said Ben, as the puppy jumped up and tried to nibble his nose.

"Oh very well," agreed Ben's dad, seeing that the two were already inseparable. "But he has to be a guard dog not just a pet."

The puppy bared his teeth and made the most fearsome and ferocious face he could.

"Oh look," said Ben, giggling. "He's smiling."

"Has he got a good bark?" asked Ben's dad,

writing out a cheque and handing it over to Mrs Walker, the lady selling the pups. She smiled broadly. "Well that's the oddest thing, he doesn't bark at all. I don't think he can."

Ben's dad was still shaking his head by the time the three of them arrived home.

"A six-inch high guard dog, with a ridiculous tail, a floppy ear and no bark," he complained to Ben's mum as she watched Ben and his new best friend race around the garden.

"Well, Ben certainly seems to like him," she remarked. And Ben certainly did.

It didn't take long for the new puppy to settle in. Ben gave him the name Jake, which sort of suited him. Jake was having the time of his life, a splendid new basket, a smart tartan collar with his name on it, an enormous garden and a wonderful family. He tried very hard to please them all, in particular Ben's dad. He handed him the hammer when he was fixing the *Beware of the Dog* sign to the gate. He hadn't meant to drop it on his toe of course, but it was rather heavy for a small dog.

He also helped in the garden doing a lot of digging and rearranging the flower beds. After that Ben's dad had been so delighted that he had shut Jake in the back porch so he could have a lovely long rest in his basket– digging was hard work, especially when you only had short legs.

And Jake did so love his basket. But, as the weeks rolled by and winter approached, it occurred to him that he might be warmer and even more comfortable if he took his splendid grey blanket and laid it on the sofa in the lounge– after all Ben's dad spent many a happy hour there.

It wasn't easy dragging the heavy blanket down the hall but eventually he managed just in time to see two men climbing in through the lounge window.

"'Ere, they've got a dog," said the first man, whose name was Stan, as he shone a torch in Jake's bewildered face.

"That would explain the sign on the gate," replied the second man, whose name was Eric, as he tumbled headfirst through the window.

"What sign?" asked Stan, who could not read.

"The one that said *Beware of the Dog*," said Eric, putting his cap back on his head.

"Nice doggie, good doggie," began Stan. He approached Jake, who cocked his head to one side and wagged his tail.

"It's okay, he's friendly," said Stan. Eric tiptoed over, but didn't see Jake's blanket strewn across the middle of the floor and fell flat on his face. Jake licked his ear. "Geroff," said Eric, trying not to laugh even though he was rather ticklish.

"Shhh," Stan said, and then pointed to a cabinet in the corner of the room. "The family silver," he added, rubbing his gloved hands together. Jake stared inquisitively at the two men. They looked rather odd in their stripy jumpers and the peculiar masks that covered

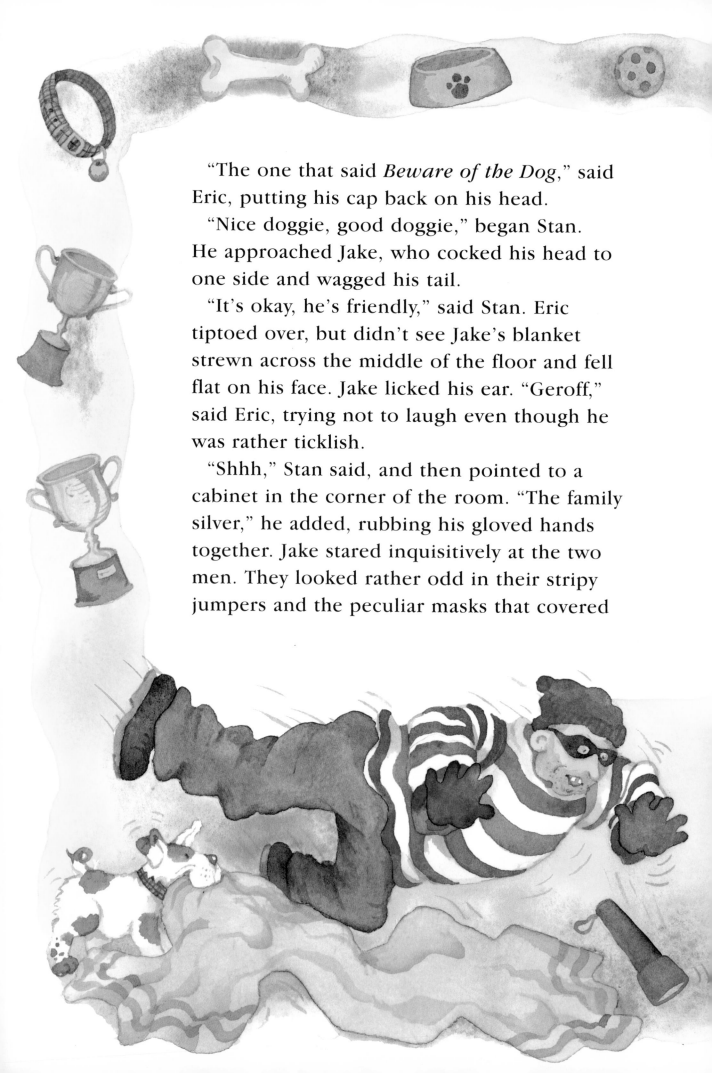

their eyes. He wanted to bark, but of course he couldn't, so he just watched as both men began to fill a large sack with Ben's dad's golf trophies. Jake instinctively knew that this wasn't right, strangers tiptoeing about in the middle of the night helping themselves to whatever they fancied. He ran towards Stan and grabbed the seat of his trousers firmly in his teeth. "Get 'im off me," said Stan in a loud whisper, but Jake would not let go. Eric grabbed the dog by his back legs and pulled and pulled until there was a rrrrr**rrrrip**.

Stan's trousers tore to reveal a pair of red and white spotted boxer shorts. Eric landed with a loud thud on the floor.

"Shhhhh…" said Stan rather too loudly, but upstairs no-one stirred.

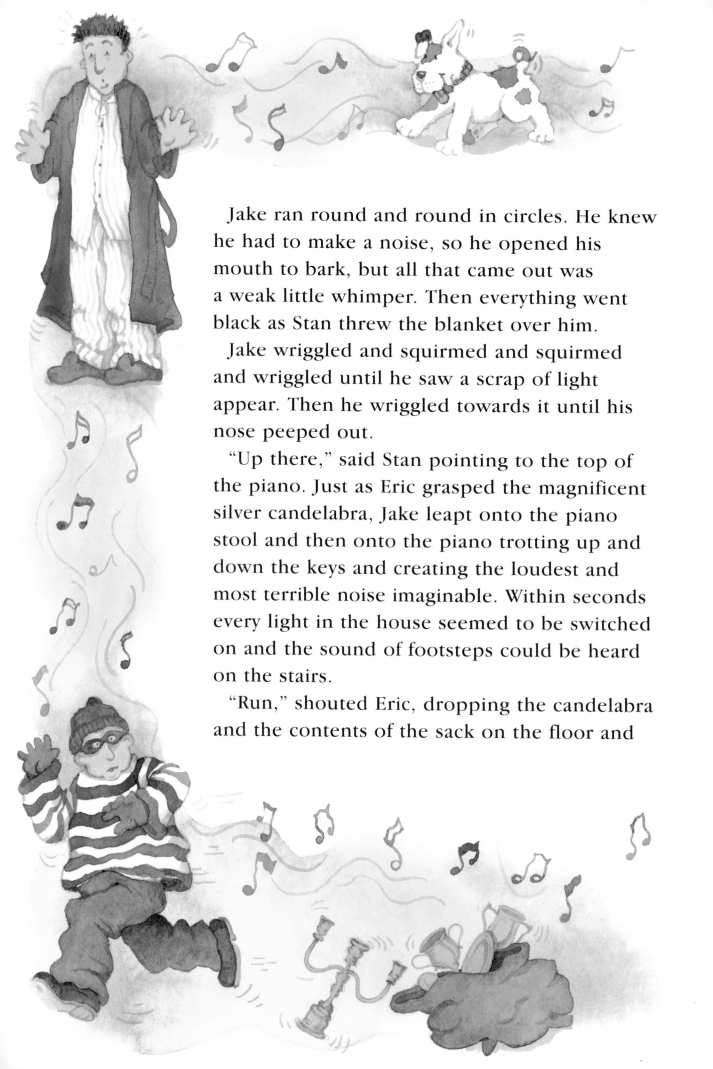

Jake ran round and round in circles. He knew he had to make a noise, so he opened his mouth to bark, but all that came out was a weak little whimper. Then everything went black as Stan threw the blanket over him.

Jake wriggled and squirmed and squirmed and wriggled until he saw a scrap of light appear. Then he wriggled towards it until his nose peeped out.

"Up there," said Stan pointing to the top of the piano. Just as Eric grasped the magnificent silver candelabra, Jake leapt onto the piano stool and then onto the piano trotting up and down the keys and creating the loudest and most terrible noise imaginable. Within seconds every light in the house seemed to be switched on and the sound of footsteps could be heard on the stairs.

"Run," shouted Eric, dropping the candelabra and the contents of the sack on the floor and

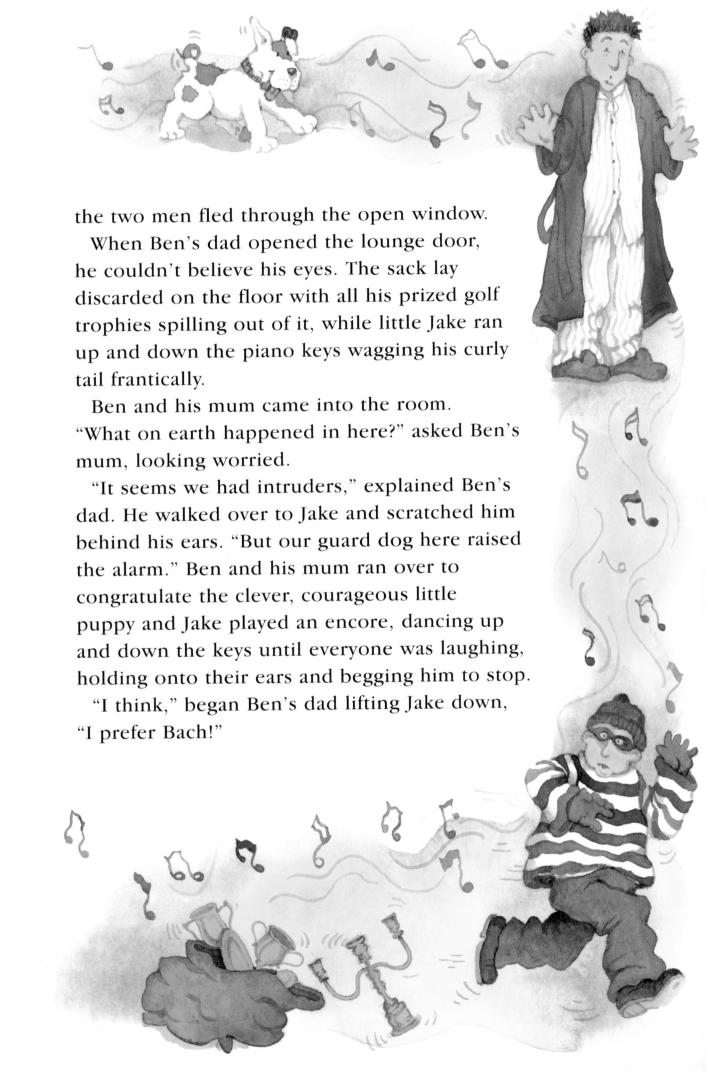

the two men fled through the open window.

When Ben's dad opened the lounge door, he couldn't believe his eyes. The sack lay discarded on the floor with all his prized golf trophies spilling out of it, while little Jake ran up and down the piano keys wagging his curly tail frantically.

Ben and his mum came into the room. "What on earth happened in here?" asked Ben's mum, looking worried.

"It seems we had intruders," explained Ben's dad. He walked over to Jake and scratched him behind his ears. "But our guard dog here raised the alarm." Ben and his mum ran over to congratulate the clever, courageous little puppy and Jake played an encore, dancing up and down the keys until everyone was laughing, holding onto their ears and begging him to stop.

"I think," began Ben's dad lifting Jake down, "I prefer Bach!"

I Wish...

I wish I was an elephant,
'Cause it would make me laugh.
To use my nose like a garden hose
To rinse myself in the bath.

I wish I was a chameleon,
Chameleons are best.
I'd change my colour and life would be fuller,
For a change is as good as a rest.

I wish I was a hippo,
A hippo's life seems good.
They don't go to school, but keep nice and cool
Messing about in the mud.

I wish I was a dolphin,
A dolphin would be my wish.
Leaping and splashing, I'd be very dashing,
And swim along with the fish.

I wish I was an ostrich,
An ostrich would be grand.
But if I got scared, would I be prepared
To bury my head in the sand?

I wish I had more wishes,
But now my game is through,
I'm happy to be, quite simply me,
Enjoying a day at the zoo.

Madame Monocle's Magic Machine

It was the king's birthday, and Quentin the royal bard had spent days preparing a birthday poem of immense length for His Royal Highness. He had searched the royal library for the perfect rhyme, for the right adjective, for the words that were guaranteed to bring His Majesty pleasure.

At last the ink was dry and Quentin was ready to read his poem to the king. The court assembled, the king took his place upon his throne and Quentin cleared his throat and began.

"To you, dear Majesty, on the auspicious occasion of your birthday…"

He began to read his verse in a loud and pompous voice. At first the king looked attentive. Then he noticed that Quentin was holding a great many sheets of paper–and was still only on page one! "Oh dear," thought the king. 'I wish I hadn't eaten so much. I'm feeling rather sleepy.' His eyelids drooped.

"...my king so fair

with lustrous hair...." Quentin was saying.

Soon the king was asleep and snoring gently. The queen was just wondering whether to wake her husband, when there was a commotion outside the throne room and in burst an old woman. She dragged a brightly painted, clattering machine behind her that made greasy black tyre prints on the marble floor as she pushed her way through the throng towards the royal throne.

"Wake up, Reggie!" hissed the queen, poking the king in the ribs with a long, red fingernail. "You must do something!"

"Eh? What? I'll teach that two-headed Martian a lesson!" shouted the king, who was dreaming that he'd been abducted by aliens. He sat bolt upright and stared at the old woman.

"Who...?" he began.

"How dare...?" started Quentin. But the old lady interrupted them both.

"I am Madame Monocle," she announced, "and this is my Magic Recycling Machine. Feed it your unwanted bits and bobs, your odds and ends, and watch them become transformed into fabulous, new and truly useful items before your very eyes!" She did a little pirouette before the king and ended with a curtsy.

The king was on the point of having Madame Monocle and her filthy machine thrown out, when he remembered how much Quentin's poem had bored him. This might be much more interesting!

The king didn't believe Madame Monocle for a minute, but he thought it would be amusing to see what happened next.

"Very well," he said. "What can your machine do?"

"What do you say we begin with a royal sock?" said Madame Monocle, reaching down to unbuckle the king's shoe. The court froze. What would the king do? Touching the royal foot was unthinkable! To everyone's utter amazement, the king sat quite meekly while Madame Monocle removed his sock, exposing five pink toes for all the world to see.

The court gasped as the old lady reached up and lifted a lid on top of the machine. In went the sock and up went a plume of purple smoke before she slammed the lid down again. Madame Monocle stood smiling sweetly as the machine began to make the most fearsome and embarrassing noises. It shook and steamed and gurgled and belched until finally out of a chute at one side slid a beautiful woollen scarf!

The king looked astonished as Madame Monocle stepped forward and arranged the scarf around his neck. Then he smiled and said, "Who else has something for recycling?"

A courtier passed the old lady a newspaper. She stuffed it into the machine and a few moments later out shot an elegant wooden candlestick. The court cheered. Everyone was fascinated by the extraordinary machine as more objects were fed into it. Everyone, that is, except for one person.

In all the excitement, nobody noticed the look of fury on Quentin's face. 'My day has been ruined!' he thought angrily. 'They didn't listen to the end of my wonderful poem! I'll make them regret it!' He slipped round the back of the machine and twiddled a few knobs. Nobody noticed. They were too busy watching to see what would come out next. Madame Monocle had just thrown a chicken bone into the machine.

All eyes were on the chute. Suddenly there was a dreadful cackling noise and out of the chute shot an old crone on a broomstick. She had a stone in her fist which she hurled straight at the king. He ducked as the stone smashed into his crown. Before anyone could stop her, the crone was away and had escaped out of the window.

"Stop the machine!" screamed the queen. But it was too late. Madame Monocle had already fed her gold ring into the machine. The contraption hissed and then began spitting out pieces of knotted old string.

There was a stunned silence. "I don't know what could have happened! It's very strange!" said Madame Monocle.

The king stood up, purple-faced with rage. "You've ruined my birthday!" he yelled. "Take her away, guards!"

"Wait!" shouted the queen. "I know your game," she continued, pointing her finger at Quentin who was smirking in the corner. "Bone, crone, stone! Ring, string! Obviously our precious court poet has turned the machine into a ridiculous rhymer!"

"Bring him here!" commanded the king. The guards, who had Madame Monocle in a tight grip, dropped their hold. They surrounded Quentin and dragged him in front of the king.

"Well?" demanded the king.

At first Quentin denied everything. But in the end he had to admit that he had tampered with the machine. He told the king how hurt he was that no-one had wanted to listen to his poem.

The king looked thoughtful. He whispered something to the queen, who thought for a moment and then nodded. Finally, he said to Quentin "Although you have greatly displeased us, nevertheless the queen and I are forced to admire your skill at producing rhymes out of this machine. As punishment, you will feed it your own work and we'll see what comes out!"

Reluctantly, Quentin fed sheet after sheet of his poem into the machine. After much whirring, down the chute came a scrap of paper with a few lines of writing on it. Quentin picked it up.

"Well?" said the king.

"It's not quite what I would have liked…" said Quentin hesitantly.

"Let's hear it anyway!" retorted the king.
Quentin arched his eyebrows and read:

There once was a young king named Reggie
Who liked cakes more than meat and two veggies
He declared, "It's a fluke
That greens make me puke,
And chops make me nervous and edgy!"

The king looked surprised. Then he burst out
laughing and so did the entire court. "Brilliant!"
he cried. "I love it! But talking of cakes – where's my
birthday cake?"

There was an awkward silence in court.
Then Madame Monocle stepped forward.
   "Perhaps I can help," she said, as she
fed a box of matches into the machine.
Hey presto – out came a chocolate cake
with candles blazing on it!
   "My best birthday ever!" beamed the
king, as he blew out his candles.

There Was an Old Lady

There was an old lady
Who lived down our street,
You wouldn't believe all
The things she could eat.

For breakfast each morning,
A full slap up meal
Of nuts and bolts served in
A bicycle wheel!

She always took care
To never miss lunch,
On brooms, mops and buckets
She'd nibble and crunch.

Trumpets and trombones were
Her favourite dinner,
But though always eating
She kept getting thinner.

For supper she'd snack on
Some bees in their hives,
All swiftly washed down with
The forks, spoons and knives!

What would finish her off
No-one could have known–
For that mad, old lady
Choked on a fish bone!